Alfred Gurney

The Vision of the Eucharist

And other Poems

Alfred Gurney

The Vision of the Eucharist
And other Poems

ISBN/EAN: 9783337206598

Printed in Europe, USA, Canada, Australia, Japan

Cover: Foto ©Andreas Hilbeck / pixelio.de

More available books at **www.hansebooks.com**

THE

VISION OF THE EUCHARIST

&c.

THE

VISION OF THE EUCHARIST

AND OTHER POEMS.

BY

ALFRED GURNEY, M.A.

VICAR OF S. BARNABAS', PIMLICO.

' Better to have the poet's heart than brain,
Feeling than song; but better far than both
To be a song, a music of God's making.
GEORGE MacDONALD

LONDON:

KEGAN PAUL, TRENCH, & CO., 1 PATERNOSTER SQUARE.

1882.

To CYRIL and WILLIE.

The father's craft I know not as I would :--
If childhood we must keep true men to be,
So more of sonship must our Father see
In those who share with Him in fatherhood.
My boys, you have one Father Who is good,
Who loves His children unforsakingly;
Your home His Bosom is, your one roof-tree
The God-revealing, Christ-uplifting Rood.
Poor verses are the best that I can make,
To higher thoughts I can but point the way,
And yet, perchance, just for a father's sake,
Your love may prize them on a coming day.
This hope, my sons, your father's heart inspires
That brighter far than his may burn your altar-fires.

WHARFEDALE, August 1881.

PREFACE.

IN DEFERENCE TO THE WISHES of a few of my friends—with great hesitation and no little misgiving—I have gathered together the following poems. They deal for the most part with very sacred and serious subjects upon which I have *felt*—I do not venture to say *thought*—deeply. The large majority have already appeared in various Reviews and Magazines. I should certainly not have sought for them a wider circulation, or entertained the idea that they possess any merit which renders them worthy of it, but for the encouragement of those to whom I should find it hard to refuse anything.

Such as they are, I offer them as a Christmas gift, first to my children, and then to my people of S. Barnabas' and my other friends. Should they reach a larger circle, it will be to me at once a surprise and a satisfaction.

ADVENT, 1881.

CONTENTS.

—•:•—

2

CONTENTS.

CONTENTS.

POEMS.

THE VISION OF THE EUCHARIST.

'Out of Sion hath God appeared in perfect Beauty.'

BEFORE Thine altars, dearest Lord,
   With prostrate hearts we fall,
We hail Thee there enthroned, adored,
   Our Jesus and our All !
The soldiers of the Cross enlist
As champions of the Eucharist.

There angel-voices ever sing
   The song for ever new ;
There Christian hearts their tribute bring
   Of praise and homage too ;
And there in prayer the faithful dead
Are lovingly remembered.

B

There dawns the smile that baffles grief,
    That vanquishes despair ;
And penitents obtain relief,
    And mourners comfort, there ;
Whose eyes discern, as clears the mist,
The Jesus of the Eucharist.

And children to the altar bring
    Their gift, they take their part ;
Methinks no sweeter offering
    Makes glad the Sacred Heart ;
Thus all extol with one consent
That venerable Sacrament.

Enkindled by the Holy Ghost
    The Pentecostal Fires
Are burning still ; how vast the host,
    How many-voiced the quires
Of Saints whose ceaseless prayers assist
The worship of the Eucharist !

Can things below meet things above ?
    Has earth so great a bliss ?
Yes ! in the Sacrament of love
    They meet and clasp and kiss ;
Where righteousness and peace embrace.
There Jesus finds a resting place.

He comes to cleanse and heal and bless,
 He comes to set us free ;
We are no longer comfortless,
 No longer orphans we ;
He comes, His promise never fails,
His word is mighty, and prevails.

So by His Spirit's gracious aid,
 And all-creating breath,
The wondrous Sacrament is made
 That shows a Saviour's Death ;
And makes His Life their life who pray
Before His altars day by day.

He spreads the Board, He makes the Feast,
 To Him our hearts we lift,
At once the Victim and the Priest,
 The Giver and the Gift ;
He veils His Majesty, that we
His brothers and His friends may be.

Our altar-veils enfold Him now,
 As erst the swathing-bands,
And there are thorn-prints on His Brow,
 And nail-prints in His Hands.
That Face, those Hands, our lips have kissed
How often in the Eucharist !

Yes ! there He ever comes to be
　　Our treasure and delight,
This is the priceless legacy,
　　This is the peerless rite,
The Gift all other gifts above,
The last invention of His Love.

'Tis thus He woos us ; He would thaw
　　The hearts made hard by sin,
Thus lifted up, He seeks to draw
　　All men, their love to win ;
That sweet constraint their hearts resist
Who disesteem the Eucharist.

Beneath the veils enable them,
　　Dear Lord, to find out Thee,
The Infant-God of Bethlehem,
　　The Lord of Calvary,
Who lovest still with men to dwell,
Whose Name is still Emmanuel.

The Word made Flesh !—this Rock indeed
　　The Church is built upon ;
Her dauntless Faith, her deathless Creed,
　　The Dogma of Saint John,*
God's Eagle, Christ's Evangelist,
Apostle of the Eucharist.

　　　　　* See Note A.

The Church of Christ renews her youth,
 Her triumphs who may tell?
The treasure-house of grace, of truth
 The rock-built citadeL
Alas! that men should still repeat
' How gives this Man His Flesh to eat?'

Yet oftentimes their hearts are true
 Whose lips the Faith deny,
A present Christ they worship too,
 And are engraced thereby.
Yes! loving hearts have seldom missed
The meaning of the Eucharist.

Of Jesu's life in Mary's womb
 How wondrous the repose!
How hushed a shrine her bosom whom
 For Spouse the Spirit chose!
A stillness no less eloquent
Encompasses the Sacrament.

The still small voice declares His will ;
 His kingdom now as then
Comes not with observation ; still
 He rules the hearts of men,
Who kneel enraptured as they list
The silence of the Eucharist.

For oh, the world no music has
   That may compare with this !
Men close their ears to it, alas,
   They know not of our bliss !
What hopes, what memories enhance
Our Eucharistic jubilance !

'Tis this that beautifies the past,
   That makes the future fair ;
The Vision we shall see at last
   That crowns the golden stair,
By which we climb the Throne of God,—
The path the nail-pierced Feet have trod.

Thus Saints have learnt the arms to wield
   That have the world subdued ;
Upon the Church's battle-field
   How great their fortitude !
The Cross uplifting high, they win
The frontier-fortresses of sin ;

Then storm the heights ; and though the strife
   Be desperate and long,
Dear Lord, Thou art the Bread of Life,
   Who feed on Thee are strong ;
Of mighty men the ranks consist
That muster round the Eucharist.

The Incarnation is the Tree
   That bears such precious fruit;
Regenerate humanity
   Strikes so secure a root
In Jesu's Manhood; fairest flowers
Attest its fertilizing powers.

And so before Thine altars, Lord,
   With prostrate hearts we fall,
We hail Thee there enthroned, adored,
   Our Jesus and our All!
For ever be the doubts dismissed
That would dethrone the Eucharist!

THE EUCHARIST A DISCOVERY OF GOD.

'Mine eyes have been enlightened because I tasted a little of this honey.'

ONE thing above all others, Lord,
    Discovers what Thou art,
To men and angels laying bare
    The secrets of Thy Heart ;
Thine all-revealing Eucharist,
    So simple, so august,
Bears witness—man is justified
    Made one with the All-Just.

Thine all-embracing Eucharist
    Is eloquent to tell
That Thou art Love, and, lover-like,
    Thou doest all things well ;
Thine all-sustaining Eucharist
    Thy Motherhood declares,*
And preaches Thy Divinity,
    And prompts Thy Church's prayers.

* See Note B.

It fills the Saints with ecstasy
  Who worship Thee above ;
It kindles in the hearts of men
  And feeds the flame of love ;
To mourners it is solace true,
  To penitents relief ;
It sweetens every human joy,
  It softens every grief.

Not only tutelage in death,
  Deliverance from sin,
The bloodless Sacrifice avails
  Repose and peace to win
For souls departed ; Death has lost
  Its terror and its sting,
Since every Eucharist proclaims
  Death's Conqueror our King.

They know the Unity of God
  In whose awakened ear
The still small Eucharistic voice
  Makes music ; for they hear
His witness Who from Both proceeds—
  The Father and the Son,
And Him to know is to discern
  That Both in Him are One.

Internal to this Unity
 Each with Each Other deals,
This life of fellowship divine
 The Eucharist reveals ;
Thou mak'st oblation of Thyself,
 O Son, unto Thy Sire,
Eternally Thy Heart enshrines
 The Pentecostal Fire.

They know the central Verity,
 Before whose lifted eyes
The Eucharistic vision dawns—
 Banquet and Sacrifice ;
' The Word made Flesh,' and ' God with us,
 Ah ! this is understood
By all who faithfully discern
 Thy Body and Thy Blood.

They know Thy Father's fatherhood
 Who at Thine altars pray,
His the self-sacrificing love
 That gives Thee day by day
To be His children's portion ; Thine
 The joy, each day renewed,
Of giving, just as mothers give,
 Thy little ones their food.

'Tis food convenient, mother's milk
  For babes—for souls mature
The bread and wine that furnish strength
  All crosses to endure ;
'Tis God's own food in sacrifice ;
  And man's true life demands,
No other food, no poorer food,
  From Thy maternal hands.

They know the meaning of Thy Cross
  Who at Thine altars kneel,
To those who know not, Lord, do Thou
  That mystery reveal ;
Thy Eucharist is eloquent
  Its virtue to declare,
The fruitfulness of sacrifice,
  The potency of prayer.

Where'er Thy priests their feet have set,
  Where'er Thy Name is known,
'Neath veils Thy Wisdom hath devise
  Thy Death is duly shown ;
Thy sinless Manhood pleads for man
  Before God's Throne on high ;
No vain appeal—Thy children live
  Since Thou hast deigned to die.

They know the Resurrection-life
   Who at Thine altars fall,
There make they the discovery
   That death gives life to all ;
There learn they with a deepening love
   The meaning of Thy Name,
For ever uttered by the tongues
   Of Pentecostal Flame.

The Eucharist is eloquent
   Thy Manhood to declare,
Divinely human is the life
   Thou manifestest there ;
That to obey is liberty
   A saving truth men find,
Since Thine obedience, Son of Man.
   Emancipates mankind.

This to Thine altar-life belongs,
   To every life of Thine ;
This is the truly human life,
   Because the life divine ;
Thy venerable Eucharist
   Proclaims it far and wide,
Of God and man the sacrifice,
   Of Bridegroom and of Bride.

Dear Lord, by all the travail-pains
   Thou on the Cross didst bear,
And by Thy Church's dauntless faith,
   And Thy prevailing prayer,
And by Thy Spirit's energy,
   And those dear words of Thine
Which make Thy Body of the bread,
   Thy Life-blood of the wine :

To me, to all, Most Merciful,
   A steadfast faith impart,
And childlike singleness of mind,
   And loyalty of heart ;
Oh may we never doubt those words,
   Of children understood,
Or deem that Thou art impotent
   To make Thy promise good !

For Thou art God, the Truth itself,
   Thy hardest words are true,
Thine Arm is mighty to perform
   What Thou art pledged to do ;
Behold the Lamb of God ! behold
   The Sacrifice for sin !
Thus worshippers without the veil
   Unite with those within.

The love Thy Eucharist enshrines
    Unceasingly renews
Its sweet appeal, though human hearts
    Its overtures refuse ;
To those who doubt Thee, Lord, and fail
    Thy presence to discern,
Reveal Thyself, till rebels yield,
    And wanderers return.

Thine everlasting Eucharist,
    ' So awful and so sweet '—
This is the bond uniting all
    Who gather round Thy Feet :
This is the grand Epiphany
    Of Thy Parental Heart ;
Thus, prostrate at Thine altar, we
    Discover what Thou art.

PONTRESINA, August, 1880.

THE INSTITUTION OF THE EUCHARIST.

'Prayer shall be made ever unto Him, and daily shall He be praised; there shall be an heap of Corn in the earth, high upon the hills.' *

O FOR a tongue made musical
　　His Goodness to declare,
Whose is the feast we celebrate,
　　Whose is the food we share!
The soul enamoured and entranced
　　Falls prostrate at His Feet,
Whose work of Sacrifice endures
　　Because it is complete.

' I will not leave you comfortless '—
　　That was His promise true,
Preluding this—' I do the thing
　　My Father bids me do;'

* See Note C.

Forthwith upon the bread and wine
His priestly Hands He laid,
And with divine, creative words
The Pure Oblation made.

Communion follows; and the while
Their hearts within them burn,
He bids His children do the same
Awaiting His return.
Then speaks He of a finished work; *
That work abideth still—
The world-redeeming Sacrifice
Of His surrendered will.†

Rejoice we in this work complete;
All that was lost is found,
We live beneath the smile of God,
We tread on holy ground;
The earth His Mercy has redeemed
Is Paradise restored;
Oh be His Clemency confessed,
His Majesty adored!

* S. John xvii. 4.
† 'Non mors sed voluntas placuit sponte morientis.'- S.
BERNARD.

All sacramental ministries
    Bring comfort to the soul,
The leper is made clean thereby,
    The sick man is made whole;
The Eucharist surpasses all,—
    Life's ever-fruitful Tree,—
The glory of Christ's presence makes
    Its dear supremacy.

Upon the holy mountain stands
    The City where we dwell,
Raised high above the shifting sands,
    A rock-built citadel.
Long since the Psalmist-seer foretold
    That high upon the hills
God's Corn should grow, and now, behold,
    His promise He fulfils!

PITLOCHRIE, September, 1877.

THE EUCHARISTIC SACRIFICE.

' In every place incense shall be offered unto My Name, and
a Pure Offering.'

God's all-sufficing Fatherhood
   The Sacraments proclaim,
Thus His dear Will is done on earth,
   And hallowed is His Name ;
The Eucharist is eloquent
   Our sonship to declare,
The children's worship it enshrines,
   The children's daily prayer.

Deep-struck, far-spreading are its roots ;
Beyond creation's bound,
   In God Himself, the living God,
   Must they be sought and found ;
The eternal Altar is the Heart
   Of God the Three in One,
And They who minister thereat
   The Father, Spirit, Son.

Love seeks its joy in sacrifice,
    It yields itself, and finds
Its being in another's life;
    It blesses whom it binds.
'Tis thus the Father loves the Son,
    Thus loves the Son His Sire;
And from Them Both the Spirit flows,
    Love's all-consuming Fire.

The Eucharistic Sacrifice
    Unveils the Life Divine,
The glory of the Face of God
    It makes around us shine;
It lifts us to that blessed Home
    Where love and peace abide,
To Jesu's Bosom it translates
    The children of His Bride.

They see fulfilled what Jacob saw,—
    Though planted on the earth
God's Ladder reaches to the world
    Where angels have their birth.
For them what Moses saw in type
    Hath its fulfilment found,
God's Burning Bush is unconsumed,
    Rooted in holy ground.

Theirs is the Whole Burnt Offering
 Which God to man hath given,
And thus is intercourse maintained
 'Twixt earth and highest heaven ;
Theirs is the Prophecy whose voice
 Grows year by year more sweet,—
He comes again, His Bride to crown,
 His triumph to complete.

Till then 'neath sacramental signs
 A hidden life He lives,
And lover-like solicits them,
 And father-like forgives ;
Thus wooed and pardoned and engraced
 His children see in part
The beauty of His Face, they hear
 The beatings of His Heart.

This Tabernacle for the Sun
 The Hand of God hath made,
And set a Rainbow round about
 Which nevermore shall fade.
The Eucharist declares His Mind,
 Makes audible His Voice,
To sinful souls it says 'Repent,'
 To contrite souls ' Rejoice.'

The Penance of Gethsemane
　　Is efficacious still,
That Agony prepares the soul
　　To climb the altar-hill ;
The Cross is still the Tree of Life,
　　Its virtue is not spent,
For all the world its fruits are stored
　　In this dear Sacrament.

O Love divine, adorable !
　　All precious things combine,
In one vast Bounty gathered up
　　'Neath veils of bread and wine.
God's all-sufficing Fatherhood
　　His children thus proclaim,
And thus His Will is done on earth,
　　And hallowed is His Name.

St. Ulrich, Tyrol., July, 1876.

EUCHARISTIC ADORATION.

'Then went up Moses, and Aaron, Nadab and Abihu, and seventy of the Elders of Israel; and they saw the God of Israel: and there was under His Feet as it were a paved work of a sapphire stone, and as it were the body of heaven in his clearness. And upon the Nobles of the children of Israel He laid not His Hand: also they saw God, and did eat and drink.'

'We all, with open face beholding as in a glass the glory of the Lord, are changed into the same image from glory to glory. even as by the Spirit of the Lord.'

THE Everlasting Doors lift up,
    And Jesus is revealed,
To loving hearts most manifest
    Where most He is concealed;
This is the Paradise of God,
    And here in glory stands
The Victim-Lamb, the Eternal Priest,
    With censer-laden Hands.

The Princes of the Church of God
    His Altar-throne surround,
As priests arrayed in robes of white,
    As kings enthroned and crowned;

The Living Creatures in the midst
 Their wondrous chant upraise,
With them we too must celebrate
 The sacrifice of praise.

The Eucharist bears witness true
 To our celestial birth,
We know, if heaven be His throne,
 God's footstool is the earth ;
The children of a Royal House—
 We too must bear our part,
One common rapture of delight
 Entrances every heart.

God's Rainbow girdles us, we kneel
 O'ershadowed by the Tree
That yields such wondrous fruit,—beneath
 Sparkles the crystal Sea ;
By its clear radiancy ensphered
 We see the sapphire stone
Flash back the golden light that streams
 From the eternal Throne.

Though high and lifted up that Throne,
 Thereto His Mercy brings
His little children as they pray,
 Anointed priests and kings.

So feast we at His Royal Board,
  So gaze we on His Face,
By His Beatitude made blithe,
  Made gracious by His Grace.

His Purity must make us pure,
  His Wisdom make us wise,
Whose Glory, seen but once of yore,
  Now lives before our eyes;
Our lips must learn His words to say,
  Our hands His works to do,
So on our resurrection-day
  Shall we be perfect too.

BRAEMAR, Nativity of B. V. M., 1877.

BEFORE COMMUNION.

'I will wash my hands in innocency, O Lord, and so will I
go to Thine Altar.'

JESU, lest we quail and falter
  As we mount the chancel-stair,
Fearing lest our hearts should palter,
  Self-deceivers e'en in prayer,
Teach us ere we seek Thine altar
  How to hail Thy presence there.

We are destitute, Thou knowest,
  Helplessness is all our plea ;
To the altar straight Thou goest,
  And Thy Smile says 'Comfort ye ;'
Thus the homeward path Thou showest,
  Thither, Lord, we follow Thee.

Thine the gracious invitation,
  Thine the Hand stretched out to bless,
Only Source of consolation,
  Only Fount of righteousness,
Come we in our degradation
  To Thy footstool for redress.

Thine the word creative spoken
  By Thy servant in Thy stead,
Thine the Body bruised and broken,
  Thine the Blood so freely shed,
Of redeeming Love the token,
  Now for us distributed.

As the woman's plague found healing
  When she laid her hand on Thee,
Oh, when at Thine altar kneeling,
  Touch us sacramentally !
As of old, Thy love revealing,
  Let us there Thy power see.

God Thou art, we would adore Thee,
  Man Thou art, we need not fear ;
God made Man, we bow before Thee,
  Word made Flesh, we Thee revere ;
By Thy promise we adjure Thee,
  Saviour, may we find Thee here !

Oh, we know still unforsaken
  Is Thy Church, Thy promise sure,
Still abides the Rock unshaken
  Which she rests upon secure,
And till all the dead awaken
  Shall Thy Eucharist endure !

Thus the Church with exultation,
   Till her Lord return again,
Shows His Death ; His mediation
   Validates her worship then,
Pleading the divine Oblation
   Offered on the Cross for men.

Lamb of God, the world's transgression
   Thou alone canst take away,
Hear, oh hear our heart's confession,
   And Thy pardoning grace convey !
Thine availing Intercession
   We but echo when we pray.

Now, dear Lord, Thy grace imploring,
   We would climb Thine altar-stair,
At Thy Feet would fall adoring,
   For Thyself our souls prepare ;
Life-imparting, health-restoring,
   May we find Thy presence there !

AT COMMUNION.

'The eyes of all wait upon Thee, O Lord, and Thou givest
them their meat in due season. Thou openest Thine Hand, and
fillest all things living with plenteousness.'

LIFE of my life, Lord Jesu Christ,
    Beneath Thy Royal Feet
I lay my heart ; Thy love alone
    Can make the bitter sweet ;
Thy love that makes the darkness light,
    That makes the water wine,
Can feed, invigorate, enlarge,
    This straitened heart of mine.

Thou fillest all the things that live
    From Thine exhaustless store ;
That Bread alone can satisfy
    Which makes us hunger more ;—
Each bounty is a prophecy ;
    To-day's dear gift bestows
A pledge that Thou wilt meet the need
    To-morrow shall disclose.

The sacramental manna falls
   With each returning morn,
When from the womb of sleep Thy Hand
   Uplifts the soul re-born ;
And new discoveries reward
   The seeker's blissful pain,
So let me seek, and seeking find,
   And finding seek again.

All that I need, who am so poor—
   All that my life demands—
Thou hast ; I lift my waiting eyes
   To Thy dispensing Hands ;
My lips still hunger for Thy kiss,
   Touched by Thy coal of fire ; *
A satisfaction ever new
   Crowns every new desire.

Lord Christ ! at length my spirit wakes,
   A child to Thee I come,
Thy sacramental presence makes
   The happiness of home ;
In Thy dear Eucharist revealed
   All-human, all-divine,
To Thine embracing love I yield
   This beating heart of mine.

NERVI, February 1878.

     * See Note D.

AFTER COMMUNION.

'I am my Beloved's, and my Beloved is mine.' 'He brought me to the Banqueting House, and His Banner over me was Love.'

Once more, dear Master, we have traced
   Thy Eucharistic Life,
Embracing Thee, by Thee embraced,
   We need not fear the strife ;
The foes who would with us contend
   Must now contend with Thee,
Who evermore dost condescend
   Thus with Thine own to be.

With us ! in us !—O loving Lord !
   Of Thine endearing ways
How dare we speak ? our hearts record
   Their best of love and praise.
Though many doubt, deny, condemn,
   Thy worshippers are we ;
Each altar is a Bethlehem,
   And each a Calvary.

And each is Patmos ; we descry
    That great Door opened wide
Through which outstreams the light whereby
    The world is glorified.
To Thee our prostrate hearts present
    The homage of their mirth,
The sunshine of Whose Sacrament
    Illuminates the earth.

Lord, make us true to Thee, we pray,
    In thought, and word, and deed,
Thy Lips that never can betray,
    That never can mislead,
Have taught us what, whoe'er assails,
    We never can unlearn—
Beneath the sacramental veils
    Thy presence we discern.

We feel the beatings of Thy Heart,
    We count Thy sorrows o'er,
Whose dying is our life, Who art
    Alive for evermore ;
Thou livest still to intercede,
    A Victim and a Priest,
Thou spreadest still, our souls to feed,
    The Eucharistic Feast.

Thus for the children of Thy Church
   Salvation's cup is full,
Her treasures, when they try to search,
   They find unsearchable ;
Thee, cradled once on Mary's breast,
   Their grateful hearts enshrine,
Possessing Thee, by Thee possest,
   They taste a joy divine.

THE EPIPHANY EUCHARIST.

A CAROL.

Let the children of Sion be joyful in their King.'

BRIGHTLY burn the tapers all,
  Fragrantly the censer swings,
Angels to each other call,
  Each a pure oblation brings ;
Children at the footstool fall
  Of the King of Kings.

Brothers, sisters, bend the knee,
  Lift the heart and bow the head ;
By this grand Nativity
  Satan is discomfited ;
Lovely should the laughter be
  In the ' House of Bread.'

See the Babe outsmiling still,
  Robed in beauty, glorified,
On the sacramental hill
  Where He loveth to abide,*
His dear promise to fulfil
  To His chosen Bride.

* Psalm lxviii. 16.

D

Here the glories are revealed
　　Which of right to her belong :
Hark ! her lips already yield
　　Preludes of the triumph-song :
For that promise unrepealed
　　Makes her glad and strong.

Learn, my soul, that song to sing ;
　　For God's mercies manifold
Make a costly offering,
　　Myrrh and frankincense and gold—
Soul and body—everything !
　　Filial love is bold.

Bethlehem is everywhere,
　　Evermore the ' House of Bread ; '
Still the star shines bright and fair
　　Which the Royal Pilgrims led
To the stable mean and bare,
　　To the manger-bed.

Mean no more, but glory-crowned,
　　Is our Bethlehem to-day ;
Thus, while angels gather round,
　　Penitents may kneel and say—
' We were lost, and we are found,
　　Therefore are we gay.'

Brightly burn the tapers all,
    Fragrantly the censer swings,
Angels to each other call,
    Each a pure oblation brings.
Keep, my soul, the festival
    Of the King of Kings.

THE EUCHARISTIC ANNUNCIATION.

'Tis silence on God's holy hill,
The place of sacrifice is still
   The place where souls are fed ;
And oh, the banqueters are blest,
In Him of all things repossest,
   Who is the Living Bread !

Of intercourse so high and sweet,
When God and man as lovers meet,
   An Angel's tongue must tell, —
The messenger to Mary sent,
The guardian of Christ's Sacrament,
   The herald Gabriel.

' The Lord is with thee ; '—still the same,
He speaks to each in Jesu's Name,
   The soul-entrancing word ;
Its sense the Spirit must unfold,
Then comes a soft reply—' Behold
   The handmaid of the Lord.'

This is the Mystery renewed
Whene'er men share the Angels' Food,
   And learn their song to sing ;
The altar still is Mary's cell,
Before it stands Saint Gabriel,
   The herald of our King.

Thus God deviseth means whereby,
His banished ones may be brought nigh,*
   From slavery released ;
Christ's sacramental advent still
Love's mighty purpose doth fulfil,
   His presence makes the Feast.

God's Church is Nazareth alway,
Where souls with Mary watch and pray,
   And love and peace abide ;
Where Jesus dwells, and angels come,
And all the blameless joys of home
   Are sweetly sanctified.

HEIDELBERG, Feast of the Holy Name, 1876.

        * 2 Samuel xiv. 14.

BAPTISM.

'He bloweth with His Wind, and the waters flow.'
'By One Spirit are we all baptized into One Body.'

CREATION is a sacrament ;
 All forms of beauty tell
Some thought that in the Mind of God
 Is most adorable ;
To all who have a loving heart,
 And a discerning eye,
He stands behind His handiwork,
 And is revealed thereby.

He bloweth with His Wind, and fast
 The cleansing waters flow,
Their sacramental energy
 The Church's children know ;
They speak of Resurrection-life
 Encompassing the earth,
And death thereby is shown to be
 God's mystery of birth.

The world, once buried 'neath the waves
    Of its baptismal flood,
Is now by living water saved,
    The water mixed with blood ;
The smitten Rock of Calvary—
    This is its fountain-head ;
Thus death gives birth to life, the Cross
    Becomes a marriage-bed.

The Virgin-Spouse of Christ conceives,
    O'ershadowed by the Dove ;
Her babes His blood-bought children are,
    Begotten from above ;
Behold the Bridegroom and the Bride !
    They twain one flesh are made,
The offspring of her virgin-womb
    Are in His Bosom laid.

With sacramental characters
    Upon their souls impressed,
He folds them in His loving Arms,
    Caressing and caressed ;
Thus is an ark of refuge found
    Upon the stormy waves,
'Tis Jesu's grace that sanctifies,
    'Tis Jesu's love that saves.

Such joys sin-stricken souls may taste
  Re-born the Font within ;
Enriched, ennobled, and engraced,
  Freed from the yoke of sin ;
The Spirit breathes, and fast and far
  The healing waters flow,
Baptizèd souls God's children are
  Whose footsteps homeward go.

THE RHÔNE GLACIER, August, 1876.

CONFIRMATION.

' Now He which stablisheth us with you in Christ, and hath anointed us, is God ; Who hath also sealed us, and given the earnest of the Spirit in our hearts.'

THE womb of waters sanctified
    Is left behind, the child
Has entered on the path of life
    Engraced and undefiled ;
But not alone,—the voice of God
    Within the soul is heard,
The Christ-child yields obedience sweet
    To His creative word.

For Christ is wrapped in swaddling clothes
    In souls re-born ; their birth
The mystery of Bethlehem
    Perpetuates on earth ; *
In them He lives, in them He grows,
    And growth and life imply
The Spirit's energy within,
    His unction from on high.

* ' Originem quam sumpsit in utero Virginis posuit in fonte baptismatis : dedit aquæ quod dedit matri.'—S. LEO.

His Confirmation brings increase
    Of sacramental grace,
Equips Christ's soldier for the fight,
    His athlete for the race ;
Enlarges the baptismal life—
    That life divinely strong,
In which the Virtues have their roots,
    To which the Gifts belong.

Whom God confirms He consecrates ;
    This Sacrament reveals
Their priestly character whose souls
    Th' anointing Spirit seals ;
O priesthood of baptizèd men,
    Sweet mystery of grace !
Thus all to service are ordained
    By Christ's renewed embrace.

For service out of sonship springs,
    Obedience out of love ;
The child, o'ershadowed by the wings
    Of the Eternal Dove,
The wisdom that has made him wise
    To brothers must impart,
And to his Father sacrifice
    A dedicated heart.

PENANCE.

'The Purification of the Sanctuary.'
'The Ministry of Reconciliation.'

How lovely are the nail-pierced Feet !
 How hot the penance-tear !
'Tis thine, O Sacrament most sweet,
 O Discipline most dear,
To teach us how to kneel beside
The Cross, how love the Crucified !

'Tis thine to teach us how to hate
 The sins that made Him die,
Thus rightly may we estimate
 Sin's fell malignity ;
To sin-sick souls in their distress
He thus reveals His loveliness.

How little Peter knew his Lord
 Ere penitence began ;
Not all untrue the caitiff-word
 'I do not know the Man ;'

Christ smote him with His Eyes, the shock
Melted to tears the man of rock.*

'Tis still the same ; those Eyes declare
  Uninjurable Love ;
The sinner, filled with self-despair,
  Their Tenderness must prove ;
So Jesus bade His Church dispense
The sacrament of penitence.

'Tis this that makes a grace of grief
  While it forbids despair,
'Tis this that fortifies belief,
  And re-inforces prayer ;
' Blest are the mourners,' Jesus said,
Thus are His words interpreted.

How blest the penitents who feel
  The sacramental touch
Of those dear Hands so skilled to heal !
  They needs must love Him much,
Whose Absolution sets them free
From sin and shame and slavery.

  * ' The rocks shall melt as wax at Thy Presence.'—Judith
xvi. 15.

'Thy sins are pardoned, go in peace'—
    So speaks that loving Voice ;
And sinless angels do not cease
    With sinners to rejoice ;
They know, who worship Him above,
Contrition is the child of love.

The child of love,—the harbinger
    Of joy that never dies ;
Methinks when Jesus looked at her
    With those love-laden Eyes,
There never was a joy more keen
Than that of Mary Magdalene.

Thine is the work, dear Paraclete,
    All perfect works are Thine ;
By this are penitents made meet
    To seek the Gift Divine,
The Gift of gifts, the Living Bread,
By Jesus still distributed.

'Tis thine, O Sacrament most sweet,
    O Discipline most dear,
To draw us to the Mercy-seat,
    Constrained by love and fear,
Where Jesus to all contrite hearts
His pardon and His peace imparts.

ORDERS.

'This Man, because He continueth ever, hath an un-changeable Priesthood.'
'As the Father hath sent Me, so send I you.'

To be, dear Lord, a hand of Thine,
A heart,—this is their work divine,
   (Be it their daily prayer !)
To whom Thine all-constraining Voice
Hath spoken, bidding them rejoice
   Thy Priestly Life to share.

To work for Thee, with Thee,—ah, this
Must be their aim, their life, their bliss,
   On whom Thy Hands have laid
A blessed and an awful thing,
The jewelled stole of suffering
   Wherewith they are arrayed ! *

* S. Basil derives the use of the stole from the cord placed on the neck of Christ in token of condemnation.

Yes ! that must be the garb of all
Who take, obedient to Thy call,
  The Priesthood's solemn vows ;
Enrich them, Lord, with grace divine,
Make tongues of flame to burn and shine
  On their anointed brows.

To shine and burn !—this task is theirs,
By fruitful lives and faithful prayers
  To keep the flame aglow,
Enkindled by the Spirit's Breath,
Till back from darkness and from death
  God's children homeward go.

How blest a work ! how great a charge !
'Tis theirs Thy Kingdom to enlarge,
  A Throne for Thee to build ;
To tune men's hearts to praise and prayer,
Until Thy Will is everywhere
  Triumphantly fulfilled.

'Tis theirs in Thy dear Name to bless
And fertilize earth's wilderness,
  A desert-land no more ;
It blooms and blossoms as the rose ;
Where'er Thy saving message goes
  Thy heralds go before.

Like bells upon Thy garment's hem,
The tongues that Thou hast given them
　　Speak as Thou drawest near ;
And sweetly, musically tell
Thy presence, though invisible,
　　To every listening ear.

O for an ever-open eye,
Quick to discern the mystery,
　　And read the lesson right
Of Love that stoops to woo and win,
Renouncing self, repulsing sin,
　　All mercy and all might !

O for an understanding heart,
To which Thy Spirit can impart
　　Those gifts we covet most,
Made fuel meet by keen desire
To feed the Pentecostal Fire
　　Lit by the Holy Ghost !

Ah, Princely Spirit ! Thine the skill
The heart to melt, to brace the will,
　　The soul to beautify !
A Christ-like life in all its strength,
In all its sweetness,—this at length
　　Must win the victory.

Bestow Thy grace, Thy gifts dispense ;
Oh, guard the avenues of sense,
   And keep our garments white ; *
Enrich our poverty, and make
Our weakness strength, for Jesu's sake,
   And all our darkness light !

Make brave and tender, pure and true,
His priests, their Master's work to do,
   Empowered from above ;
And all mankind at length shall see
That Priesthood means fraternity,
   Self-sacrifice, and love.

ATHENS, June, 1875.

   * Ecclesiastes ix. 8.

MARRIAGE.

'This is a great mystery: but I speak concerning Christ and the Church.'

'The head of every man is Christ; and the head of the woman is the man; and the head of Christ is God.'

SWEET is the sound of marriage-bells,
    And blithe the bridal song,
And deep the joy of wedded hearts
    Whose love is pure and strong;
Love springing from a common root—
    The love of Him who came
To reinstate humanity
    Released from sin and shame.

Fair shone the sun on Cana's feast,
    The guests were glad and gay,
When Jesus and His Mother came
    One happy wedding-day;
His presence made the festival,
    His Hand dispensed the wine;
And marriage, blest by Him, becomes
    A sacrament divine.

He blesses all, transfigures all :
 Thus womanhood is blest,
Anointed for a priestly work,
 No longer dispossest ;
Her heart love's tabernacle is,
 Her knees the altar, where
The new-born babes of God are taught
 To lisp the children's prayer.

All lives He lived : the virgin-life
 His Life hath glorified ;
Yet, Virgin though He be, He reigns
 The Bridegroom of the Bride.
His Natures' holy wedlock speaks
 Of God's eternal plan,
Who, stooping o'er His sleeping child,
 Took woman out of man.

Man slept in ecstasy—he waked,
 And on his opening eyes
There dawned a face love-lit, aglow
 With rapturous surprise ;
His heart discerned the gift of God,
 His image and his spouse,
The crown of perfect womanhood
 All-radiant on her brows.

' God gives to His Belov'd in sleep.' *
    So sleeping on the Rood
(Strange death-sleep, while th' unsleeping heart
    Yields water mixed with blood !)
The Second Adam bows His Head,
    And from His opened Side
The Sacraments are drawn that make
    The life-blood of His Bride.

Thus vaster grows the mystery,
    More clear the shadows fall ;
Discerning eyes detect therein
    God's writing on the wall ;
And loyal hearts are quick to own
    The presence of their King ;
Love-tokens, God's forget-me-nots,
    They find in every thing.

His Voice makes sweet the marriage-bells,
    Makes blithe the bridal song,
And His the joy of wedded hearts
    Whose love is pure and strong,—
Love springing from a root divine,
    In His dear Love made fast,
Who still turns water into wine,
    And keeps the best till last.

CORTINA, TYROL, July, 1876.

* Psalm cxxvii. 3. This is, I believe, the true meaning.
The psalm has been attributed to Solomon.

UNCTION.

'There is treasure to be desired, and oil in the dwelling of
the wise.'

'The house was filled with the odour of the ointment.'

'O GRAVE, where is thy victory?
　O death, where is thy sting?'
So round the dying child of God
　The blessed angels sing;
The sick-room has its sacrament,*
　The consecrated oil
Declares His presence, Who is sent
　The spoiler to despoil.

For Christ is still the Healer, still
　To touch His garment's hem,
With hands outstretched, the sick folk come,
　And He recovers them.
Or dying they inherit life;
　Sweet angel of release—
Death puts a limit to their strife,
　And bids their sorrows cease.

* See Note E.

The holy oil prevails to teach
  All souls that will be taught,
That life and death are Christ's, and each
  With wondrous blessings fraught.
' O Jesu, Thou art strong to save,
  A Conqueror, a King ! '
Thus, round the death-bed and the grave,
  The happy angels sing.

CHRISTMAS EVE.

'Repent, prepare '—each Advent morn
  So speaks the Church's voice,
'Twill say, when Christmas Day shall dawn
  As urgently ' Rejoice ; '
For still His glory God conceals,
  That we may share his joy,
Still Bethlehem's bright star reveals
  The Mother and the Boy.

And still we make that pilgrimage,
  And on that stable-floor
Rejoice with shepherd and with sage
  To kneel and to adore ;
And still the Mother's bliss we share
  As every Christmas morn
Each altar is the manger where
  The Holy Babe is born.

And soon the Babe becomes the Man,
   He suffers and He dies,
And still the sinless Life we scan,
   The perfect Sacrifice ;
And still our Jesus is the same,
   And still He grows more dear,
And still the world-redeeming Name
   Is music to the ear.

His Voice is in the plaintive wind,
   'Tis in the tuneful sea,
Its tones are sweet, its accents kind,
   It whispers 'Come to Me,
All ye who suffer, ye who mourn,
   With griefs and toils oppressed,
The weak, the weary, the forlorn,
   And I will give you rest !'

Still, wheresoe'er the shadow falls,
   Of some o'erwhelming grief,
When sin affrights, and death appals,
   And nothing brings relief,
Then think we of the Love revealed
   In Jesu's dying breath,
With blood the testament is sealed
   That disinherits death.

So think we of the Crib, the Cross,
    The Mother, and the Boy ;
He makes a gain of every loss,
    Of every grief a joy ;
Oh, there's a magic in His Smile,
    A music in His Voice,
He comes to reign and reconcile,
    Let all the world rejoice !

1870.

EASTER EVE.

(*In Memoriam G.A.G.*)

WHEREVER Christians lay their dead
  They build the Holy Sepulchre,
  They bring the spices and the myrrh,
Like her to whom the angel said—

' The Lord is risen ; ' then like her
  They see the great stone rolled away,
  Their load of grief, and know that they
Have found a Strong Deliverer.

Across death's valley comes that voice,
  ' The Lord is risen ; ' we can tell,
  Since Jesus doeth all things well,
Why weeping mourners should rejoice.

Yon sun so bright, when day is done,
  Is lost in the Atlantic waves ;
  But earth, which has so many graves,
Has still a Sunrise and a Sun—

The Sun that dawned at Bethlehem,
   Eclipsed at Calvary, to shine
   More brightly still with light divine,
That gilds a thorny diadem.

Our Easter Sun ! so warm, so clear,
   That weeping mourners cease to weep,
   And stricken souls revive ; we keep
The resurrection of the year.

Oh, blessings on the months that bring
   The primrose and the violet,
   When all the groves are song-beset,
And sorrow's a forgotten thing !

Oh, blessings on the Spring that makes
   All Christian hearts with Paschal mirth
   So blithe ; they hail His second Birth,
Whose Love pursuing ne'er forsakes !

He lives who died ; He lives to bless,
   He lives to cleanse and heal and save :
   A shrine is every Christian grave,
A garden is earth's wilderness.

Day follows night ; sweet Summer brings
   (Though deathful Winter tarry long)
   Her warmth and fragrance, mirth and song,
When all creation laughs and sings.

And Christian hearts rejoice ; our eyes
  Discern the Risen Christ, we know
  To suffer is to share His woe ;
Since He has risen, we shall rise.

Wherever Christians lay their dead
  They build the Holy Sepulchre ;
  And sweetly rests each slumberer,
No longer disinherited.

1873.

FROM CHRISTMAS TO EASTER.*

MIGHTY Mother, Spouse of Jesus,
    When thou mak'st the Saving Sign,
Earth outblossoms into heaven,
    Water blushes into wine,
All things straightway are transfigured
    By thy ministry divine.

Led by thee we journey homeward,
    Taught by thee we win the fight,
Thine the mighty arm that shields us
    On the left hand and the right,
Thine the voice that softly whispers—
    'Walk by faith and not by sight.'

Poets sing of happy childhood,
    Tell of youth's unclouded joy,
Yet methinks more lasting pleasures
    Bless the man than did the boy,
Joys more full of satisfaction,
    Hopes less easy to destroy.

*· Part of this poem will be found in 'Christmas Carols,
New and Old,' by Bramley and Stainer, 3rd Series, LVII.

Bright the rainbow-tints of boyhood
  In the holiday of life,
When each face with smiles is dimpled,
  Every voice with laughter rife,
Sweet the dream of great achievements
  Compassed in the coming strife.

Oh, the world is full of wonder
  That the eyes of youth behold !
And to youthful ears its music
  Is that talisman of old,
Which, when Orpheus touched the harp strings,
  Savage beasts and birds controlled.*

But another spell is needed
  When the pulse of youth is strong,
When on boyhood's mind converging
  Vain imaginations throng,
And the passions fiercely surging
  Sweep their torrent-course along.

* ' For Orpheus' lute was strung with poets' sinews,
   Whose golden touch could soften steel and stones,
   Make tigers tame, and huge leviathans
   Forsake unsounded deeps to dance on sands.'
      SHAKESPEARE, *Two Gentlemen of Verona*, Act iii.

Then thy voice my ear detected,
 Whispering in accents mild,
' Watch and pray, my son, that holy
 Be thy youth and undefiled ;
Lo ! 'tis Christmas Day, and Christmas
 Brings to us a little Child.'

Hence my soul, herself uplifting,
 Through the midnight watches dim
Kneels beside the Holy Manger
 With adoring Cherubim,
Till from them and thee, dear Mother,
 She has learnt the Christmas hymn.

' Now to God on high be glory,
 And to men on earth be peace,'—
'Tis the Eucharistic anthem,
 Music that shall never cease,
To a ransomed world proclaiming
 Jesu's advent, man's release.

Christendom at all her altars
 Once again the tale doth tell
Of His Birth, Who came to vanquish
 Sin and Satan, Death and Hell,
Virgin-born, and Manger-cradled,
 God with us, Emmanuel.

Now, through all her fanes resounding,
　　Once again the trump is blown ;
Once again the holy Yule-tide
　　Makes the happy tidings known ;
Once again all Christian people
　　Kneel beside the Manger-throne.

See the shepherds, heaven-greeted,
　　Worship while the Angels sing ;
See the Magi, star-directed,
　　Their most costly treasures bring :
See earth's simple ones and wise ones
　　Bending o'er their Baby-King.

Happy Mother, Ever-Virgin,
　　Mary clasps Him to her breast,
All succeeding generations,
　　Speaking of her, call her blest,
And Saint Joseph joins with wonder
　　In the homage of the rest.

Saviour ! by Thy love and pity,
　　Tried so oft and proved so well,
By the victory that vanquished
　　Sin and Satan, Death and Hell,
Make us sharers in Thy triumph,
　　Jesu, our Emmanuel !

Now, dear Lord, Thy Birth-day keeping,
   As we bend before the shrine,
Find Thee life and health bestowing,
   Veiled beneath the bread and wine.
Make us like Thee, child-like, God-like,
   Keep, oh keep us ever Thine !

Keep me Thine ! oh, may I never
   Cease to offer up that prayer !
Great the risks that wait on boyhood,
   Manhood also has its share ;
Doubt, the foe that now assailed me,
   Came, the herald of despair.

All life's mystery had vanished,
   All life's melody was hushed,
For I felt my faith was blighted,
   And I knew my hopes were crushed ;
Like a wanderer benighted
   Through the wilderness I rushed.

'Twas the desert in life's journey
   Where so many lose the way,
See by night no flaming column,
   And no pilot-cloud by day,
With the Promised Land before them,
   Learn to doubt and disobey.

Yet with milk and honey flowing,
   Still that Land its wealth displays ;
God with His rebellious children
   Deals in many gracious ways,
Turning curses into blessings,
   And defiance into praise.

For that voice, once more appealing,
   Came as it had come before,—
' Rise, what mean you thus repining ?
   Rise, and trust Him evermore,
Who (behold 'tis Easter morning !)
   Rises now a Conqueror.'

Wakes my soul, herself uplifting,
   All her blessedness foretells,
Finds her downward course arrested.
   Listening to the Easter-bells ;
Then a larger faith emboldens,
   And a deeper love impels.

For the gladsome Easter-sunlight
   Supersedes her Lenten gloom,
Burst upon her ears the tidings
   ' Christ is risen from the tomb,'
Risen, her Emancipator
   From the darkness and the doom.

Two days since the Cross was lifted
    On that memorable hill,
Lifted the appointed Victim
    Her redemption to fulfil;
Now, though risen and triumphant,
    See ! His Wounds are open still.

Open still His Heart, inviting
    Love responsive; dearest Lord !
Kindle answering devotion
    In the souls Thou hast restored;
Be Thy Majesty exalted !
    Be Thy Clemency adored !

As to-day we kneel adoring
    Where the altar-tapers shine,
Hail the covenanted presence
    Veiled beneath the bread and wine,
See we in Good Friday's Victim
    Christmas morning's Babe Divine.

See we Him Who with the Father
    From the first was glorified;
His the thorn-encompassed Forehead,
    His the mutilated Side,
His the Hands and Feet nail-tortured,
    And the piercing Voice that cried—

'Father, pardon them, they know not
    What they do ; '—and 'It is done ; ' *
Death-stained, sin-crushed, interceding,
    See we there the Sinless One,
See we, crucified and bleeding,
    There the Sole-begotten Son.

Christendom at all her altars
    Tells the wondrous tale to-day
Of the Resurrection-triumph,
    And the great stone rolled away,
And the Sepulchre deserted,
    Where the Lord of glory lay.

Christ is risen ; rise we with Him,
    Through Him, to the life divine ;
He can baffle this world's sadness,
    Making all its water wine ;
He can read life's riddle—only
    Love and patience must combine.

Every gift and every blessing,
    All the wealth of sea and land,—
All we are, and have, and hope for,
    More than we can understand,—
All good things in earth and heaven
    Reach us from the nail-pierced Hand.

        * Apocalypse xvi. 17 ; xxi. 6.

And of noble aspirations
   Every age has had its share ;
Still the voice is raised in blessing,
   Still the head is bowed in prayer,
Still in self-renunciation
   Men will suffer and will dare.

Still the world is full of music,
   Still survives the saintly line,
Still in God's recovered garden
   Grow the palm-tree and the vine,
Where a sick world's wounds are gaping,
   Yielding oil and yielding wine.*

All the things I loved in boyhood—
   Still I love them more and more,
But in most of them a meaning,
   That I never found before,
Turns my wonder into homage,
   And to love is to adore.

Past the rapids in life's voyage,
   Broader, deeper grows the stream.
Bright the rainbow-tints of boyhood,
   Youth's intoxicating dream ;
Ah, but words must fail to utter
   How divinely fairer seem

     * S. Luke x. 34.

Those that mix with manhood's sunshine !
   (Mother, thou canst tell my joy !)
Yes, indeed, more lasting pleasures
   Bless the man than did the boy,
Joys replete with satisfaction,
   Hopes that nothing can destroy !

Mighty Mother, Spouse of Jesus,
   By thy ministry divine
Sweetly all things are transfigured,
   Earth is heaven, water wine ;
Thou for Christ didst bear, dost feed us,
   Thou art His, and we are thine !

PENTECOST.

'Where the Spirit of the Lord is there is liberty.'
'As many as are led by the Spirit of God they are the sons
of God.'

WHERE dwelleth God's Spirit there Freedom abides,
And the Catholic Church over which He presides
Is the Mother of freemen ; they only are free
Who consent, who rejoice His disciples to be.

His clients, His pupils, His subjects, they share
In the life of the Mystical Body, and there,
Where He dwells without measure and works without
   pause,
'Tis their joy, 'tis their pride, to submit to His laws.

The Eternal Embrace of the Father and Son,
In Him, the Third Person, They ever are One ;
They share in a common Spiration, and this
Is His Double Procession, Their mutual bliss.*

* 'Quòd Pater et Filius se mutuò amant, oportet quòd
mutuus amor, qui est Spiritus Sanctus, ab utroque procedat.
Secundum igitur originem Spiritus Sanctus non est medius,

'The Word was made Flesh,'—thus a Temple was built
Wherein He could dwell uninvaded by guilt;
And thus is accomplished God's marvellous plan,
And the Spirit of God is the Spirit of man.*

The Church is Christ's Body made visible still,
Its law is the Spirit's adorable will,
That law supersedes every other, and they
Are as free as the wind who acknowledge its sway.

It is Thine, Re-Creator, the grace to impart
That awakens the conscience, that softens the heart;
The manifold workings of grace in the soul
It is Thine to originate, Thine to control.

All lessons Thou teachest,—most precious by far,
Men have learnt what the joys of discipleship are,
Of service, of sonship,—a Father's sweet name
Filial lips, filial hearts Thou hast taught to proclaim.

The health-giving Sacraments,—these too are Thine,
Thy Table is furnished with Bread and with Wine,
Thy Grace is a strengthening, gladdening Oil;
No foe can defeat Thee, no robber despoil.

sed tertia in Trinitate Persona.　Secundum verò prædictam
habitudinem est medius nexus duorum ab utroque procedens.'
S. Thomas Aquinas.　And he quotes S. Augustine :—' Spiritus
Sanctus est quo genitus a generante diligitur ; genitoremque
suum diligit.'
　　* See Note F.

Revive then Thy work in the midst of the years,
Enkindle high hopes, put to flight rebel-fears,
The Standard Thou liftest, empurpled with blood,
Can alone rout the foe that comes in like a flood.

May the fruits of Christ's Passion abound more and
      more,
May the cloven tongues speak in the Church as of
      yore,
That Church is Thy Palace, Thy children are we,
'Tis the House Thou hast built, 'tis the Home of the
      free ! *

THE CEDARS OF LEBANON, Whitsuntide, 1875.

* ' Ubi Ecclesia ibi Spiritus.'—S. IRENÆUS.

CONVERSION OF S. PAUL.

ALL the triumphs of grace, dearest Master, are Thine,
The rock yields its water, the water-jars wine,
At Thy word of command.   Oh, we thank Thee for all
That Thou gavest Thy Church in the gift of Saint Paul!

What conquests were his! what a wondrous campaign!
Through Asia, through Europe,—Greece, Italy, Spain,
The standard of Jesus he carried unfurled,
And he claimed for his King nothing less than the
        world.

The Gentiles' Apostle—we all have a claim
To call him our father, to cherish his name ;
Engraced and converted, to each comes the call
To walk in the steps of Christ's hero Saint Paul.

So hard seemed his heart as he stood by unmoved,
And saw how the faith of Saint Stephen was proved,
Unshamed he beheld his death-throes, his last breath,
By his life unconvinced, unconcerned at his death.

That breath—it was weighted, 'twas winged with a
    prayer
That soon found its answer,—we know how and where.
As he drew near Damascus his pride had a fall,
And Saint Stephen obtained the conversion of Saul.

It is grace that prevails, it is love that subdues,
Oh, surely 'tis hard their appeal to refuse,
To kick 'gainst those pricks, to be deaf to that Voice,
And not to choose Him Who has made us His choice !

Even now with their backs on Jerusalem turned
There are those who Christ's loving entreaty have
    spurned,
And, breathing out slaughter, delight to proclaim
Their hatred of all who are called by His Name.

May the words strong and sweet that arrested Saint
    Paul
Be spoken, dear Lord, in the hearing of all
Who in blindness and wrath and fanatical zeal
Are deaf to Thy Church's beseeching appeal.

In love take them captive, in love cast them down,
Then show them Thy Face,—'tis a smile, not a frown,
That shall woo them and win them, so radiantly bright
As to dazzle and darken their eyes with its light.

So blinded and humbled, their souls shall receive
The grace Thou bestowest; they too shall believe :
And the scales from their eyes thus anointed shall fall,
And their hearts shall be Thine like the heart of Saint
      Paul.

DAMASCUS, Whitsuntide, 1875.

THE INVENTION OF THE CROSS.

AH ! when the Cross is found and known
    All things are viewed aright,
Upon life's scenery is thrown
    A golden glory-light.

Till this discovery is made,
    All treasures sought and found
Are like the flowers doomed to fade,
    Uprooted from the ground.

All men are seekers ; happy they
    Who fare upon this quest,
Seeking the priceless Cross alway
    Until it be possest.

Till they their need of this confess
    The eyes of men are sealed ;
Life's awfulness, life's blessedness,
    To them are unrevealed.

But when at length the Cross is found,
　Straightway anointed eyes
Discern Love's Victim glory-crowned—
　Divine Self-Sacrifice!

Another, truer Cross they see
　Bound to that Cross of wood ;
The world-redeeming Cross must be
　A Cross of flesh and blood.

A mystery doth this declare
　The Father's Heart within ;
Behold ! the Cross is planted there,
　His protest against sin ;—

To sinners His appeal ; when this
　At length is understood,
The Cross is found to be the kiss
　Of yearning Fatherhood.

Only when that is seen and known
　Can things be viewed aright ;
A scaffold makes a glory-throne,
　And thorns a crown of light.

Who find the Cross must carry it :
　So doing they are blest,
By salutary toil made fit
　Beneath its shade to rest.

GLENCOE, September 1880.

A MODERN PILGRIMAGE.

1.

Oh, hapless is his lot who lives
  Our modern life with little men !
  The golden age comes not again,
And life nor peace nor pleasure gives.

For hushed are all sweet sounds by those
  That jar upon the tortured ear ;
  We suffer from a constant fear,
An utter absence of repose.

Oh, happy, when the world was young,
  Were men who lived a peaceful life !
  They knew not of our modern strife,
Or how to prostitute the tongue.

They lived among their flocks and herds
  With simple wants and homely ways,
  And fruitful was their length of days,
Grave were their thoughts, and wise their words.

Now words of wisdom seldom flow
    From human lips, the fevered brain
    Is restless, but a nameless pain
Forbids to fructify and grow.

The world a garden was of old,
    Nor weed nor brier grew therein,
    Nor death had access there, nor sin,
But God's good gifts were manifold.

The world still wore its baby-smile,
    Not yet oblivious of the Hand
    That fashioned it, adorned, and planned
A thousand wonders to beguile :

The wonders dimly understood
    By Adam when he walked with God,
    What time the new-born earth He trod,
Pronouncing all things very good.

Where may we now His foot-prints trace?
    We nothing see save pain and sin,
    Distress without us and within,
And God-forsaken seems our race.

For blind our eyes, our souls are blind,
    If God there be, we know Him not,
    And all uncomforted our lot,
We seek, but scarcely hope to find.

II.

Too well we know our own distress,
    And how uncomforted our lot ;
    If God there be, we know Him not,
We share not in His blessedness.

For man his garden-home hath lost,
    And, when the day is cool, no more
    He walks with God as erst, before
This shipwrecked world was tempest-tost.

And yet there have been some, we know,
    Not all unblest who trod this earth,
    And now and then the angels' mirth
Hath found an echo here below.

Unless the Bible-writers lie,
    Bright angel-feet have passed, 'twould seem,
    'Twixt earth and heaven ; Jacob's dream
Revealed no unreality.

And once a voice of thunder broke
    The silence, when to Sinai's crown
    In Self-disclosure God came down,
And all the mountain-echoes woke.

'Those ancient fables but endure,'
   I hear you say in quiet scorn,
   'To grace, embellish, and adorn
An old, outlandish literature.

'For men were children once, and then
   They suffered from credulity ;
   But modern thought is bold and free :
Faith is for children, not for men.'

And yet, sin-burdened, wounded, crushed,
   I find small comfort in your word ;
   And earth, methinks, can ill afford
To have her sweetest music hushed.

Not all, not quite untrue perchance
   Those ancient fables ; here and there
   God may have heard a good man's prayer,
And showed a gracious countenance.

And one day, haply, we may find
   Not all forsaken is our race ;
   Though still averted be His face,
It is not otherwise than kind.

III.

If God be kind, if God be good,
    Yet would it not enhance our weal,
    Unless He made His children feel
The sonship born of fatherhood.

Old prayers, old psalms we oft have read,
    Which seem (and dare we call them blind ?)
    The words of those who thought mankind
Still God-beloved and governèd.

We hear of men who knew Him well,
    Had with Him dealings manifold,
    And how they worshipped Him, we're told,
Nor found Him inaccessible.

'Ho ! every one that thirsteth, try
    This stream, for you its water flows,
    On you a Father's hand bestows
The dainties wealth could never buy.'

So spake a prophet once, a sound
    Most grateful to a famished world,
    And Heaven's banner was unfurled
For helpless men to rally round.

' The Lord my Shepherd is, and I
    Need fear no want ; ' so sang the king
    Whose youth was spent in shepherding
His father's flocks so heedfully.

You say faith is not to be prized
    In men ; yet, whether false or true,
    Methinks no evil can accrue
From words so sweetly harmonized—

From words whose music finds a way
    To hearts enfeebled by despair—
    Methinks strong words of praise and prayer
Can do no harm, whate'er you say.

We gather comfort, courage, strength,
    From all that breathes a hope so sure,
    A trust so dauntless, such secure
Repose in arms divine.   At length

We hear a prophet-voice foretell
    (But this 'twere folly to believe)
    ' Behold, a Virgin shall conceive,
And call her babe Emmanuel.'

IV.

'Behold, a Virgin shall conceive,
    And bear a Son, and call His name
    Emmanuel, and on the same
The ransomed nations shall believe.'

So runs the strange announcement ; yet,
    Although the reason may rebel,
    I hear a whispered voice ' "Twere well,
Before that message you forget,

' The claims to sift and scrutinize
    Of Him they call the Virgin-born :
    If so uncomforted, forlorn,
'Twere worse than folly to despise—

'"Twere worse than madness to reject
    Whatever offers you redress ;
    His voice perchance is raised to bless,
His arm is lifted to protect.'

It may be so ; I feel, if this
    Be false, 'tis vain to search for truth,
    Uncheered is age, unblest is youth,
Death hath no hope, and life no bliss.

I can no other creed embrace,
          No other creed of love displays
          Such wealth ; oh ! how I long to gaze
In rapture on a human face—

A face that is divine as well,
          A face I could not doubt or fear,—
          And such a face confronts me here,
Of such the Gospel-stories tell.

They tell of One whose hand could heal ;
          They tell of One whose love-lit eyes
          Were full of tender sympathies ;
Of One whose princely heart could feel—

Could bleed for all, howe'er distressed ;
          Of One whose all-commanding voice
          Could bid despairing men rejoice,
And mock them not when thus addressed.

My darkness, Lord, illuminate,
          If light there be, Thou art the light,
          Assist my spiritual sight,
Oh, pity my forlorn estate !

v.

To Thee the darkness and the light
    Are both alike ; I well may wait
    Till Thou my darkness dissipate,
And clear my spiritual sight.

Enough to know that Thou hast trod
    This earth, and re-created all ;
    I hear Thy Voice, I heed Thy call,
I know Thee now, my Lord, my God.

I hear about my path, my bed,
    The words our Lady heard, ' All hail,'
    I call to mind the wondrous tale
Of Mary, Angel-visited.

I call to mind the Virgin-birth,
    The Manger-cradle, and the Rood ;
    O Virgin-born, from Thee all good
Proceeds in heaven and in earth !

For unto us a Child is born,
    To us a Son is given, Who
    The world beneath Him shall subdue,
He is the Day-star, His the dawn—

The dawn which to my night succeeds,
　　When rises in my heart the star
　　That heralds day, and from afar
The storm-vexed spirit homeward leads—

The home which in Thine Arms I find,
　　There, only there, my Lord, my King
　　To sheep long lost and wandering
Thou art a Shepherd good and kind.

Dear Saviour, I have wandered long
　　Amid distractions and alarms,
　　I felt not Thine encircling Arms,
I did not know that they were strong—

Strong to deliver, strong to raise
　　The fallen, to emancipate
　　The captives ; Jesu, all too late
With rapture on Thy Face I gaze !

The Face whose smile hath beautified,
　　Whose lips have blessed a world undone,
　　Of ransomed Christendom the sun,
Thy Church's solace and her pride.

VI.

Dear Lover of the souls of men,
    Still let me feel Thy guiding Hand,
    And things I scarcely understand
Become intelligible then.

Thou wast made man to re-create,
    Ennoble, ransom, beautify,
    And sharing Thy Humanity,
By mysteries immaculate—

Thy healing sacramental touch—
    Conveyed, imparted, we possess
    Capacity for holiness
Within the Church Thou lovest much.

The Church ! Thy Life Incarnate still
    Extended and prolonged, Thy Spouse,
    Ta'en from Thy Side, what time Thy Brows
Were thorn-enclosed on yonder hill

As Eve from Adam ;—so the Blood
    And Water from Thy Side became
    The Church's life, and through her frame
Still flows a sacramental flood.

Her foes are many ; there are those
    Who worship self and mammon, worse
    Than heathen ; others boldly curse
Their Maker,—they are open foes.

But subtler ones there are whose voice
    Proclaims aloud one half her creed,
    The other half, they dare to plead,
Accords not with their wilful choice.

And so her seamless robe is rent,
    And marred her beauty, and her crown
    Is taken from her.   Lord, look down !
On Thee her bleeding brows are bent.

Dear is my Mother Church, whose womb
    Hath borne me, at whose tender breast
    I gather strength ; oh, may I rest
Beneath her blessing in the tomb—

Which is the gate of Holy Land,
    And Thou, to Whom the souls of men
    Are precious, wilt be with me then,
And I shall surely understand !

Lent, 1868.

A GREAT QUESTION.

'When the Son of Man cometh, shall He find faith on the earth?'

CHRIST'S question through the ages rings
   Unanswered by His Lips ; His Eyes
   Hold in their light of love replies
To all our silent questionings.

Ah ! silence is a sepulchre
   Where faded lips wax eloquent ;
   The question asked was surely meant
To make each soul a questioner.

Those silent Wounds, so dear and dread,
   Are all the answer that we need ;
   He is the Father's Word indeed,
So all things are interpreted.

Of old dwelt faith upon the earth ;
   Men walked with God, in daily toil
   Conversed with Him ; who dares despoil
Mankind of rights that come from birth?

'What rights?' the scoffer asks ; I say
  'Birthrights ;' my Father's child, with Him
  I live my life ; my light is dim,
But hope anticipates the day

When, in the light of love revealed,
  All questions shall be answered, then
  Shall God be justified of men.
Alas ! for those who will not yield ;

Whom love repels, whose caitiff-hearts
  Will no home-courtesies fulfil,
  Rebellious to a Father's Will,
Rejecting what His Hand imparts.

Must, then, the children's ranks be thinned ?
  God grant that on a coming day
  These too might tread the homeward way,
Confessing ' Father, we have sinned.'

Then would He fold them to His Breast,
  Aweary of their wandering,
  And blithely would the angels sing—
'The lost are found, and all are blest.' *

From Manger, Cross, and Sepulchre,
  Christ's question through the ages rings ;
  His children of all questionings
Discern in Him the Answerer.

CAMPO SANTO, PISA, February, 1878.

     ' See Note G.

THE VISION OF THE SEVEN SEALS.

Apocalypse VI. 1–12 and VIII. 1.

First Seal.

' And I saw when the Lamb opened one of the seven seals,
and I heard one of the four Living Creatures saying as with a
voice of thunder, Come and see.   And I saw, and behold a white
horse; and He that sat on him had a bow ; and a crown was given
unto Him; and He went forth conquering and to conquer.'

Dear Conqueror ! the white horse bears Thee now,
As erst the ass's foal on Olivet ;
Now on Thy Head a golden crown is set,
Where once the twisted thorn-branch bound Thy Brow.
Radiant Thy Face, once bathed in bloody sweat ;
No reed Thy Hands clasp now, a lover's bow
Whose arrows wound, and wounding, health bestow.

Second Seal.

' And when He opened the second seal, I heard the second
Living Creature saying, Come and see.   And there went out
another horse that was red ; and power was given to Him that
sat thereon to take peace from the earth, and that they should
kill one another ; and there was given unto Him a great sword.'

Thou art the God of battles ; red Thy horse
Whose hoofs strike fire, and double-edged Thy sword ;
Till wrong be righted, harmony restored,

A blood-stained path must be Thine onward course.
Hero of heroes, as of lords the Lord !
The war Thou wagest drives false peace away,
And thus inaugurates God's Sabbath-day.

THIRD SEAL.

'And when He opened the third seal, I heard the third
Living Creature saying, Come and see. And I beheld, and lo!
a black horse; and He that sat on him had a pair of balances
in His Hand. And I heard a voice in the midst of the four
Living Creatures say, A measure of wheat for a penny, and
three measures of barley for a penny ; and see thou hurt not the
oil and the wine.'

Thou art the Judge, and black the horse whose rein
Thy left Hand grasps ; Thy right Hand holds on high
A pair of balances, and stern the cry
Uttered by those who follow in Thy train,
And quote the famine-prices.   Must we die ?
A voice replies, with clemency divine,
' Hurt not the oil of grace, of truth the wine.'

FOURTH SEAL.

'And when He opened the fourth seal, I heard the voice of
the fourth Living Creature saying, Come and see. And I looked,
and behold a pale horse, and His Name that sat on him was Death,
and Hell followed with Him.   And power was given unto Him
over the fourth part of the earth, to kill with sword, and with
hunger, and with death, and with the beasts of the earth.'

The pale horse bears Thee, Lord, of death the Death,
By whose strong Hands e'en Hell is captive led ;
We see our foes all numbered with the dead,

All deadly things Thou slayest with Thy Breath,
Thy royal Foot is on the serpent's head.—
Still speak the Living Creatures, ' Come and see
How rides our Warrior-King to victory ! '

FIFTH SEAL.

' And when he opened the fifth seal, I saw underneath the
Altar the souls of them that were slain for the word of God and
for the testimony which they held ; and they cried with a loud
voice, saying, How long, O Lord, holy and true, dost Thou
not judge and avenge our blood on them that dwell on the
earth?   And white robes were given unto every one of them.'

With happy trembling, and with holy fear,
Beneath God's Altar white-robed souls await
The further opening of the opened gate,
The brighter vision of His Face so dear,
Whose final triumph they anticipate.
And this the burden of their wistful song—
' How long, O Lord? O conquering Lord, how long ? '

SIXTH SEAL.

' And I beheld when he opened the sixth seal, and lo! there
was a great earthquake, and the sun became black.'

All things must needs be shaken, darkness still,
When travail-pangs assail, broods o'er the earth.
So only living things attain their birth,
As erst upon the Cross-surmounted hill
God's anguish was the prelude to His mirth.

That holy mirth a stricken world shall share
As love begets the hope that slays despair.

SEVENTH SEAL.

'And when He opened the seventh seal, there was silence
in heaven about the space of half an hour.'

God's thunder brings the silence, makes the peace.
Earth's noise comes only from the jaws of hell ;
To this—to all that jars—we say farewell
When Jesus bids the storm its raging cease,
And brings us home to His own citadel.
That citadel no tempests ever shake,
And naught but music can its silence break.*

* There is a French proverb full of meaning,—' Le bruit est si
fort, qu'on n'entend pas Dieu tonner.'

THE CITY OF OUR SOLEMNITIES.

'Thou shalt be called Sought out, a City not forsaken.'

THE Tree that grew on Calvary,
 With arms far-stretching, still
O'ershadows Christendom, alas !
 No city on a hill ;
On Prophets and Apostles built,
 Christ the chief Corner-stone,
The Church, divided, sore beset,
 Still is not overthrown.

Within are fears, for Christian men
 Against each other rise ;
Without are fightings, for the world
 Its Saviour still denies ;
It hates that mystery of woe,
 The thorn-encompassed Face,
It cares not for salvation's wells
 Of sacramental grace.

H

The Sacred Presence unwithdrawn
  Convinces it of sin,
It knows itself, though fair without,
  All rottenness within ;
It dreads the vengeance long delayed,
  It dreads His Judgment-throne,
Who from the Cross administers
  A kingdom not its own.

I know not if for England's Church
  Still darker days impend,
The foes are many, and but few
  The citadel defend ;
Yet still our God is pitiful,
  The Saints are strong and wise,
And wield a weapon which the world
  May hate, but not despise.

For still is heard in English fanes
  The voice of daily prayer,
And still the daily Sacrifice
  Is duly offered there
At English altars, where the lights
  Symbolically show
His presence, Who, the world's true Light,
  Still tarries with us so.

He tarries, though with rebel-hearts
    And sacrilegious hands
Bad men insult Him as of old,
    Yet still the promise stands—
‘With you alway, while lasts the world,
    It is My will to be,’—
‘This is My Body—Offer this
    In memory of Me.’

And some there are whose tears o’erflow,
    What time their hearts beat high,
Resolved for Christ alone to live,
    Prepared for Him to die ;
They know the world’s profound distress,
    The Church’s ills they know,
And higher beat their hearts, what time
    Their tears the faster flow.

Lord ! may Thy Church, upraised once more,
    Subdue the hearts of men,
And may a Pentecost transform
    Thy Christendom again ;
And be Thy Name confessed by all,
    Thy Cross uplifted high,
Until a ransomed world repeat
    The anthems of the sky !

All things are Thine, to Thee are due
    The services of all,
And Thou wilt graciously accept,
    And gently disenthral ;
Thou only canst emancipate,
    Who art Thyself the Truth,
Thine be the thoughtfulness of age,
    The hopefulness of youth ;

Thine be the strength and energy
    Of manhood in its prime ;
Thine be the toil of hand and head,
    Of every age and clime ;
The Church claims everything for Thee,
    Recovers every loss,
Her merchandise she brings from far,*
    Her trade-mark is the Cross.

Dear Saviour ! make our hearts to burn,
    And make our lives to shine,
Oh, make us ever true to Thee,
    Aud true to all that's Thine—
Thy Church, Thy Saints, Thy Sacraments,
    Thy Scriptures ; may we own
No other Lord, no other rule,
    But Thee and Thine alone !

       * Proverbs xxxi. 14

In Thine own time, in Thine own way,
  The prayers shall be fulfilled,
Which importune Thee day by day
  Our Sion to rebuild ;
And though our days be dark, and though
  That time we may not see,
A priceless blessing waits, we know,
  On loyalty to Thee.

RAVENNA, Passion-tide, 1869.

SONG FOR A BAPTISMAL BIRTHDAY.

WHEN I was born, when I was born,
   I know not whether fear or hope
   Presided o'er my horoscope,
'Twas early on a rainy morn
     That I was born.

When I was born, when I was born,
   Scarce had stern Winter given place
   To gentle Spring, whose comely face
Still looked embarrassed and forlorn,
     When I was born.

When I was born, when I was born,
   Perchance she fancied some distress
   Might wait upon her loveliness,
Some cruel blight retard her dawn,
     When I was born.

When I was born, when I was born,
   Dark turned to light, and dull to bright,
   Day stood upon the corpse of night,
And laughed to celebrate the morn,
     When I was born.

When I was born, when I was born,
  Blithe Spring, where'er her feet were set,
  With snowdrop, primrose, violet,
Proclaimed herself no more forlorn,
      When I was born.

When we are born, when we are born,
  Tearful the joy, subdued the mirth ;
  But oh, how bright that Second Birth,
When in the Font to serve we're sworn
      The Virgin-born !

When we are born, when we are born,
  We pass from darkness into light ;
  When wanes life's day, a second night
Conducts us to another morn,
      In Heaven born !

S. Moritz, Engadine, 1868.

A MAY-DAY SONG. *

'Behold thy Mother.'

THE happy birds *Te Deums* sing,
   'Tis Mary's month of May,
Her smile turns Winter into Spring,
   And darkness into day ;
And there's a fragrance in the air,
   The bells their music make,
And oh ! the world is bright and fair,
   And all for Mary's sake.

Where'er we seek the Holy Child,
   At every sacred spot,
We meet the Mother undefiled,
   Who shun her seek Him not ;
At cloistered Nazareth we see,
   At haunted Bethlehem,
The throne of Jesus, Mary's knee,
   Her smile, His diadem.

* See Note II.

The Daughter, Mother, Spouse of God,
  None silence her appeal,
Who long to tread where Jesus trod,
  What Jesus felt to feel ;
O Virgin-born ! from Thee we learn
  To love Thy Mother dear,
Her teach us duly to discern,
  And rightly to revere.

To love the Mother, people say,
  Is to defraud the Son,
For them, alas ! there dawns no May,
  Until their hearts are won ;
Then when their hearts begin to burn—
  Ah, then, to Jesus true,
And loving whom He loves, they learn
  To love Saint Mary too !

How many are the thoughts that throng
  On faithful souls to-day !
All year we sing our Lady's song,
  'Tis still the song of May—
Magnificat—oh, may we feel
  That rapture more and more !
And chiefly, Lord, what time we kneel
  Thine altar-throne before.

'Tis then when at Thy Feet we pray
    We share our Lady's mirth,
Her joy we know who hail to-day
    Thy Eucharistic Birth,
That trembling joy to Mary sent,
    Ah, Christians know it well,
With whom in His dear Sacrament
    Their Saviour deigns to dwell !

Yes ! Mary's month has come again,
    The merry month of May,
And sufferers forget their pain,
    And sorrows flee away,
And joys return, the hearts whose moan
    Was desolate erewhile
Are blithe and gay once more, they own
    The charm of Mary's smile.

Thy Son our Brother is, and we,
    Whatever may betide,
A mother, Mary, have in thee,
    A guardian and a guide ;
Thy smiles a tale of gladness tell
    No words can ever say ;
If but, like thee, we love Him well,
    The year will all be May.

' All hail ! '—an Angel spake the words
    We lovingly repeat,
The song-notes of the singing birds,
    They are not half as sweet ;
This is a music that endures,
    It cannot pass away,
For Mary's children it ensures
    A never-ending May.

ARGELÈS, May 1870.

THE WORSHIP OF BEAUTY.

WHEN youth and health crown Beauty's head.
    Unvisited by sorrow,
When Beauty, gay and garlanded,
    Recks nothing of to-morrow ;

When Beauty's pulse is beating high,
    And Beauty's cheeks are roses,
When Beauty never breathes a sigh,
    Except what Love imposes ;

When Beauty gaily plays her part,—
    All music, mirth and motion,—
Then Beauty may subdue the heart,
    Constraining its devotion.

But Beauty, when her eyes with tears
    Are full to overflowing,
When Beauty, with advancing years,
    Finds Grief a friend worth knowing ;

When Beauty's pulse is beating low,
   And Beauty's bloom departed,
When Beauty tries to smile, although
   Bereaved and broken-hearted ;

When Beauty nobly plays her part,—
   Devotion, resignation, —
Then Beauty must constrain the heart
   To yield her adoration.

DAY-DREAMS.

'Dreams are true while they last, and do we not live in dreams?'—TENNYSON.

DAY-DREAMING oft I seem to see
    The pleasant park, the winding lane,
    And live those happy days again
When Sybil used to ride with me.

One tiny hand controlled the rein,
    One dainty foot the stirrup pressed,
    And proudly arched the chestnut's crest,
And gaily danced the chestnut's mane.

A rosebud nestled at her breast,
    Whose hue her dimpled cheek would wear
    When re-adjusting fallen hair,
Which wanton breezes had caressed.

My dreams still picture her as fair
    As when my heart stood still to feel
    One little word of hers must seal
My fate ;—it came—the word 'despair.'

Ah, Sybil ! time can never heal,
  The wound that you inflicted then ;
  How many of my fellow-men
As sad a secret could reveal.

Some droop awhile, reviving when
  They find them other lips to kiss,
  But Sybil, let me tell you this—
Some droop, and ne'er revive again.

A LOVER'S SONG.

In the school of Love we find
Much to discipline the mind ;
Learn we, as the years pass from us,
Loving, still to be resigned ;
    Smiling, sighing,
    Living, dying,
Strength be ours, for ever trying
Love's high duty to fulfil.

In the voice of Love we hear
Tones that justify the fear
Lest what once was dearly cherished
Should not always be held dear ;
    Laughing, weeping,
    Sowing, reaping,
Faith be ours, for ever keeping
Loyal heart and steadfast will.

In Love's conduct should we see
What betokens jealousy,
What might bring, if uncorrected,
  Love's self into jeopardy ;
    Sleeping, waking,
    Giving, taking,
Grace be ours, for ever making
  Trustfulness more trustful still.

Lady, should it be confessed
One there is who loves thee best,
'Mid the royalties of beauty
  Finding thine the queenliest ;
    Hoping, fearing,
    Still revering,
Loveliness so all-endearing,—
  Lady, should you take it ill ?

A WEDDING GIFT.

Love makes a joy of everything ;
   She heals the wound, she rights the wrong ;
She visits with her comforting
   The lovers who have waited long ;
Her voice it is that bids me sing
   This little marriage-song.

And yet I know not how to sing
   All that my heart would wish to say;
As pledge of love I can but bring
   One little flower, if I may ;
Accept the homely offering
   Which at your feet I lay.

I plucked it in a garden where
   So many wondrous flowers grow,
And all are fragrant, all are fair—
   The Bible-garden ! and you know
The flowers never wither there ;
   Our Lord has made it so.

Take, then, this word-flow'r ; it upgrew
  O'ershadowed by the Living Vine ;
Say if it be not sweet and true,
  Almost a sacramental sign ;
Such as it is I give it you—
  ' Love makes the water wine.'

TO MY SISTER.

'A countenance in which did meet
Sweet records, promises as sweet.'

WORDSWORTH.

SWEET Sister, with the lips that pray,
And with the smile that scares away
   Despondency and doubt,
And eyes so dark and yet so bright,
So radiant with unearthly light,
   Theirs is the witchery of night,
   When moon and stars are out.

Thy like I never yet have seen,
Thou art not quite a fairy-queen,
   Nor yet an elfin-sprite ;
More like a beautiful princess,
Whose every smile is a caress,
   Whose voice is musical to bless,
   Yet that thou art not quite.

The fairy-queen would laugh at us,
The elf would be so mischievous
   And as for the princess—

As tender-hearted she might be,
Her eyes might smile as lovingly,—
Methinks she'd hardly be as free
    From all self-consciousness.

I picture thee in every guise,
As Summer suns and Winter skies
    Alternate smile and frown ;
'Tis always Summer in thy heart,
And thou to others dost impart
Its glow ; *to me thou ever art*
    A queen without a crown.

And yet a triple crown is thine,
Which seems all others to outshine
    To me comparing them ;
The hand that ever sows the seeds
Of loving thoughts and words and deeds
A sceptre holds ; my Sister needs
    No other diadem.

All beauty is of love the cause,
Who doubt it disallow her laws,
    And desecrate her shrine.
Oh ! had I but a poet's fire,
One hand at least should sweep the lyre,
To sing thy praise I would aspire ;
    Such honour should be thine

As theirs who used in days of yore
By minstrel or by troubadour
    To have their praises sung ;
Like Dante, passionate, austere,
With whom to love was to revere ;
Thus Arthur worshipped Guinevere,
    When chivalry was young.

Such in my thoughts the place you hold,
One of a sisterhood enrolled
    Whose names are very dear ;
All worthy of a poet's kiss
As were the lips of Beatrice,
When to her paradise of bliss
    The Florentine drew near.

And more than that ; I picture thee
One of the white-robed company,
    More dear than all beside,
Whose names I never can forget,
Whose memories are fragrant yet,
Cecilia, Agnes, Margaret,
    Brides of the Crucified.

Such are my thoughts ; nor only that—
I hear thee sing *Magnificat,*
    And can but think the while

How all of beautiful and good
(If rightly loved and understood)
In girlhood and in womanhood
    Blends with our Lady's smile.

Sweet Sister, with the praying eyes,
So loyal to the sanctities
    That banish doubt and fear,—
Dear eyes, so dark and yet so bright,
So radiant with unearthly light,
Theirs is the witchery of night,
    When moon and stars shine clear !

TYNTESFIELD, February 14, 1870.

TO MY BROTHER.

OBIIT IN FEST. S. BARNABÆ, MDCCCLXIX.

Requiescat in pace.

ANOTHER voice is sweetly hushed,
   Another pulse is still,
Another face withdrawn, whose smile
   Made sunshine on God's hill ;
The grave-stones where our hearts have wept
   Are mile-stones on the road
By which, a pilgrim band, we climb
   The citadel of God.

Dear Brother, when thy prayers ascend
   For me before the shrine,
And when (it is a daily prayer)
   I plead for thee in mine,
As we approach a common Lord,
   The thought is very sweet —
Unbroken is their fellowship
   Who at the altar meet.

I kneel before the Sacrament,
    And creed and hymn and prayer
Proclaim the Church's dauntless faith
    That God Himself is there ;
And saints and angels bow the head
    Before His altar-throne,
Who, ever loyal to His word,
    Thus tarries with His own.

And thou art His ;—Oh, who can say—
    What words can ever tell—
Their peace of mind who hear the voice
    That whispers—' All is well !'
'Tis then I feel how near thou art,
    Thy face I almost see,
When in the Eucharist I touch
    The Hand that touches thee.

And He Who now has welcomed thee
    This blessing did ordain,
That thou on earth should'st taste with Him
    The sacrament of pain ;
A wondrous privilege was thine
    So near the Cross to stand,
And gaze upon the thorn-bound Brow,
    And clasp the nail-pierced Hand.

Across thy path a shadow fell,
    A shadow from the Rood,
And hence thy sweet serenity,
    Thy gentle fortitude ;
And patience had her perfect work
    When bodily distress
Had formed in thee the mind of Christ,
    So strong in feebleness.

And when thou stood'st confronting death,
    Thy feet upon the brink
Of that dark stream, the thought of which
    Makes trembling nature shrink,
Thou didst not know a moment's fear,
    No doubts assailed thee then,
So certain of His deathless love
    Who lives the King of men.

He passed the threshold of thy room,
    He stood beside thy bed,—
The Vanquisher of sin and pain,
    The Raiser of the dead,
The Healer of humanity,
    Of blind, and deaf, and dumb,—
When priestly hands dispensed for thee
    The sweet Viaticum.

He came not then to raise or heal,
　But, as thine eyes grew dim,
To take thee, folded to His Heart,
　To fall asleep in Him.
Thus glory blossoms out of grace,
　Thine eyes are dim no more,
Thy soul has found its native place
　On the eternal shore.

The angels of the Sepulchre
　Seem evermore to sing—
'O Grave, where is thy victory?
　'O Death, where is thy sting?'
Death dies beneath the Hands of Christ;
　And, Brother, thou canst see
That Face, the sunrise of the world,
　Ah, it is well with thee!

SLEEP AND DEATH.

'In a dream, in a vision of the night, when deep sleep falleth upon men, in slumberings upon the bed ; then He openeth the ears of men, and sealeth their instruction.'

'Whether we wake or sleep, we shall live together with Him.'

'There shall be no night there.'

FORTH from the sepulchre of sleep
  With each returning morn we come,
  God's hand uplifts us from that tomb,
His eyes unwearied vigil keep,

Till scattered by the rising sun
  The shadows flee ; though dark and dim
  The paths we tread, we know to Him
The darkness and the light are one.

So sweet is sleep, a prophecy,
  With each returning fall of night,
  That Death, the harbinger of light
And life, shall find us by-and-bye.

The Lord is shepherding His sheep,
  In every danger their defence ;
  Sleep signifieth confidence,
And death is life-renewing sleep.

God sings His children's lullaby :
  Who trust His father-love may rest
  Of all divinest things possest ;
To doubt Him is indeed to die.

Lord, slay my doubt, my darkness slay,
  In Thee no darkness dwells at all,
  And I am Thine whate'er befall,
My night must flee before Thy day.

THE GRACE OF TEARS.

'Jesus wept.'
'Blessed are they that mourn, for they shall be comforted.'

STRONG Son of Man, of men the King,
Now to Thy Heart my heart would sing,
   Now to anoint Thy blessed Feet
Joy-tears shall be my offering.

Ah, Lord ! what tears Thine Eyes have wept !
Across Thy radiant heavens swept
   A rain-storm, when two sisters showed
The tomb wherein their brother slept.

Yet all the tears by mourners shed
To laughter are transfigurèd,
   If in Thy bottle they be stored
Whose love prevails to raise the dead.

And blessed are the hearts that mourn,
For deepest joy is sorrow-born ;
   To furnish forth the Feast of feasts
We crush the grape and bruise the corn.*

       * Isaiah xxviii. 28.

The gracious tears that fill the eyes
Of penitents, when they arise
   Absolved by Thee, are pearls that gem
The shining gates of Paradise.

So to Thy Heart my heart would sing ;
Though worthless be the best I bring,
   Thy dear acceptance gives a worth
To it, to me, to everything.

PORTO FINO, Sexagesima Sunday, 1879.

S. VERONICA.

A LOVELY tale, misunderstood
 By those who fail to see
The earth o'ershadowed by the Rood,
 The world a Calvary.

All feet the blood-stained path must tread,
 By which the goal is won,
Up which the Father's Spirit led
 The cross-encumbered Son.

Mothers are there by Mary's side,
 The cross their hearts within ;
Strong men, like Simon, glorified
 By painful discipline ;

And consecrated virgins, too,
 Whose eyes with tears are dim,
The Master's footsteps still pursue,
 And minister to Him.

So she of whom the legend tells,
   The type and pattern stands
Of virgin souls, whom love impels
   To serve Him with their hands.

Though but a handkerchief she bring
   To cool His aching Brows,
His graciousness the offering
   Right gratefully allows.

Right royally He deigns to be
   Indebted to her care ;
Straightway His generosity
   Anticipates her prayer.

One word, one smile ;—He makes her whole,
   He lays her heart to rest ;
Methinks it was upon her soul
   His image was impressed.

TYROL, September, 1880.

K

'THE GOLDEN STAIR.'

(A PICTURE BY E. BURNE JONES.)

God's children tread life's Golden Stair,
 A pilgrim-band descending slow ;
 Though sorrowful, they seem to know
A secret that forbids despair.

Hushed is their music, for as yet
 Their path descends ; in penitence
 They seek the Master's footstool, thence
Arising, they their feet shall set

More firmly on His Stair of Gold
 In glad ascent ; no words can tell
 The Majesties invisible
Their eyes are destined to behold.

Meanwhile their lovely silence makes
 Loud lamentation for their sin ;
 Till one who holds a violin
With lovely sounds the silence breaks.

The Cross it is that in her hands
   Responds to their unuttered prayer ;
   Each maiden on the Golden Stair
Its gracious message understands.

And now the Doves of God are seen
   O'ershadowing the Stair of Gold,
   And on one side of it, behold !
The Tree of Life, God's Evergreen.

And over all a radiant dawn
   Gives promise of a Golden Day ;
   The pilgrim-maidens go their way
No longer silent and forlorn.

And here the painter pauses, here
   'Tis well for all to pause and wait ;
   The sequel I anticipate
Painter nor poet can make clear.

Changed is the scene ; they climb, they sing .
   Sweet is the song that celebrates
   The opening of the Golden Gates
To happy pilgrims entering.

Learn thou, my soul, the Cross to bear,
   Leave thou the things that are behind,
   And Godward climb,—thou too shalt find
The path of life a Golden Stair.

THE RHINE AT COLOGNE.

FROM age to age the river flows
   From Alpine heights to northern seas ;
It finds its cradle amongst those,
   Its sepulchre with these.

A lordly river, swift and strong,—
   'Twas once a babbling baby-stream :
Full grown 'tis silent, and its song
   Has passed into a dream.

Its journey was begun in haste,
   Laughing and leaping it arose,
Unmindful of the salt sea waste,
   The grave to which it flows.

But here a larger, sadder stream,
   Not unpolluted are its waves ;
To share the sorrows it would seem
   Of towns whose walls it laves.

It hears the speech of every land,
   It lends itself to every keel,
If men its voice could understand
   What could it not reveal !

It gathers burdens as it goes—
   The Nations' mighty water-way ;
What secrets would its depths disclose
   Brought to the light of day !

Yet are there some who understand :
   They see its waters mixed with blood,—
A guardian of the Fatherland,
   A minister of good.

Past busy towns, past silent graves,
   Down-lapsing ceaselessly it flows,
Unconscious of the hungry waves,
   The tomb to which it goes.

It bids the fruitful vineyards grow
   More fruitful still by night and day,
It shares the toil of man, and so
   It goes upon its way.

On, on, the ancient river flows
   Between the hills, beneath the trees ;
At length its music finds a close
   Lost in lamenting seas.

COLOGNE, September, 1880.

OBER AMMERGAU, 1871.

A MOUNTAIN stands whose lofty brow,
   The Cross uplifting high, recalls
   The altar-hill ; its shadow falls
Athwart the roofs of Ammergau.

Fond memory will linger long
   About those highland homes, and where
   That village church invites to prayer,
And love is keen, and faith is strong.

In shifting groups the peasants mix,
   Saluting as to Mass they go ;
   Unlettered folk, how well they know
The language of the Crucifix !

The Church their Mother, they are blest :
   The Church their Teacher, they are wise ;
   Wisdom makes bright their Teacher's eyes :
And love makes warm their Mother's breast.

So taught, the things unseen they see,
  The things they see they ponder well ;
  So taught, those peasant-voices tell
The oft-told tale of Calvary.

With praying lips, and eyes that pray,
  And hearts that worship, they prepare
  To preach their solemn sermon,—prayer
Makes eloquent their Passion-Play.

The work of loving hearts whose fire
  Is kindled at the altar ; thence
  Comes that impassioned eloquence,
The preaching of that peasant-quire.

May we, too, at the altar kneel ;
  Thus, only thus, can we discern
  God's secret ; thus alone we learn
The lessons of the Passions-Spiel.

Her net the Church spreads far and wide ;
  And mistress still of head and heart,
  The home of Truth, the school of Art,
She preaches Jesus Crucified.

Grateful my heart shall ever be
  To Ammergau, still lingering where
  Those awe-struck peasants kneel in prayer
Around their wondrous Calvary.

OBER AMMERGAU, August, 1871.

OBER AMMERGAU, 1880.

The Cross a Tree of Life I see,
  The centre of a ransomed world,
  The banner that was first unfurled
By wounded Hands on Calvary.

The Cross, Thy sceptre, staff, and rod,
  Rules, comforts, disciplines the hearts
  Of men, and evermore imparts
The knowledge of Thy Heart, O God.

Nine years have passed, and once again
  A passion-pilgrim here I kneel,
  Thankful for what the years reveal,
And for the gladness born of pain.

These nine long years of widowhood
  To me a deepening joy have brought :
  Lord, Thou art found in sorrow sought.
In darkness Thou art understood.

And this is life eternal ; this
   Suffices,—Thee to find and know,
   To love and worship ; only so
We pass from bitterness to bliss.

The Cross exhibits grief, and yet
   'Twas joy that led Thee to that goal ;
   The man who seeks to be made whole
On Calvary his feet must set;—

That Mount of myrrh and frankincense,
   Where sweetness, born of bitterness,
   Brings comfort to the heart's distress,
Yields solace for the soul's suspense.

The Cross discovers grace and sin ;
   Of sin the malice, and of grace
   The virtue to destroy all trace
Of leprosy the soul within.

The Cross discovers death and life,
   Life born of death, death doomed and slain.
   And rapture superseding pain,
And victory succeeding strife.

The Cross is still Thy staff and rod,
  Thy blood-stained banner still unfurled,
  Revealing to a ransomed world
The secrets of Thy Heart, O God.

OBER AMMERGAU, September, 1880.

ALEXANDRIA.

THIS was the city, here the place
  Where Mark first came the Cross to rear,
  And build a throne for Christ ; and here
The royal-hearted Athanase,--

The Saint, all sweetness and all strength,—
  Did battle with the impious lie,
  The Christ-dethroning blasphemy,
And won the victory at length

Which gladdens still the hearts of all
  Who love the world-redeeming Name.
  With pride let Christian lips proclaim
His praise who helped to build the wall

That guards the Church's citadel.
  To Christ, the Giver of all grace,
  Be thanks for brave Saint Athanase,
And for the Creed he loved so well.*

          * See Note I.

And here another champion rose,
  That priceless Creed to vindicate,
  Upon this throne Saint Cyril sat,
A terror to the Church's foes.

And many another name beside,
  Wise Clement, lofty Origen,—
  Theirs is the honour due to men
Whose intellect is sanctified ; *

Who dedicate with duteous care
  To God the gifts received from Him,
  Who see, when other eyes are dim,
Truth's countenance so grave and fair.

Though dead, their works do follow them,
  Fruits of the ever-fruitful Cross ;
  Though all things suffer change and loss,
Unfading is their diadem.

Lord, hear the weeping prayers of men
  Who yearn to see upraised, unfurled,
  The Standard of a conquered world,
Thy Cross ! oh, plant it here again,

* See Note K.

Where died Saint Mark, where toiled so long
   Thy great Confessor Athanase ;
   Re-flood with Pentecostal grace
Thy Church ; dear Lord, redress her wrong !

ALEXANDRIA, January, 1875.

BETHLEHEM.

'A little child shall lead them.'

THE music of the angels' hymn—
　It has not died away,
From many a shrine those strains divine
　Are wafted day by day.

Where'er a Christian altar stands,
　Our Bethlehem is there ;
And morn by morn the Christ is born,
　We find Him everywhere.

How priest-like was the Mother-Maid
　When first her Child she kissed ;
How mother-like the priestly hands
　That clasp the Eucharist !

Yes ! Bethlehem, 'the House of Bread,'
　This is our home, and here,
Where shines the star, the wise men are,
　And pastoral spirits dear.

Here souls erst dark and desolate,
    Abandoned and alone,
Their sorrows past, repose at last
    Beside the manger-throne.

Here hearts grown old regain their youth,
    Since Mary's Babe has smiled ;
And all things sweet together meet
    Around the Eternal Child.

His Name is still 'the Prince of Peace,'
    He comes our joy to be;
And birthdays bright owe all their light
    To His Nativity.

And souls bereaved, confessing now
    That death has lost its sting,
He can beguile, His baby-smile
    Transfigures everything.

His Birth it is that conquers death,
    His Life that conquers sin ;
And oh ! how blest are all who rest
    Those infant-arms within !

They share His triumphs and His joys,
    He makes His goods their own ;
The world for them is Bethlehem,
    An altar and a throne.

His Hands still multiply the loaves,
    Still make the water wine ;
Salvation's sacramental wells
    O'erflow with grace divine.

The grace is His, and His the throne
    Established now on earth,
From under which the waters flow
    Of our baptismal birth.

Out of the mouths of very babes
    Has God ordainèd strength ;
And from the Strong all sweetness comes *
    This Man-child born at length.

After a night of travail sore—
    A weary, weary night—
His beauty all-consoling is,
    All-conquering His might.

* Judges xiv. 14.

He bids us share His throne with Him,
    And wear His diadem ;
He seeks a cradle in our hearts,—
    Ah, this is Bethlehem !

Man's heart has learnt the angels' mirth,
    His lips their hymn—their creed,
Since Jesu's birth makes all the earth
    A Bethlehem indeed !

BETHLEHEM, April, 1875.

CALVARY.

'The Tree of Life, which is in the midst of the Paradise of God.'

STILL stands the Cross, the saving Cross,
    It stands for evermore,
So mighty to repair our loss,
    Our sonship to restore.

Where'er a Christian altar stands,
    Our Calvary is there ;
Upheld we see the wounded Hands
    In sacerdotal prayer.

The world's High Priest it is Who prays,
    His words are strong and few ;—
' Father forgive ' is what He says,
    ' They know not what they do.'

The once-slain Lamb confronts our eyes,
    We own Him God and Lord,
In sacramental mysteries
    By filial hearts adored.

Earth's altars—are they not the feet
  On which that Altar stands,
Where Jesus hath His glory-seat,
  A sceptre in His Hands?

His priestly Heart still intercedes—
  A world-redeeming prayer !
His priestly work endures ; He pleads
  For all men everywhere.

Thus heaven and earth one Temple make,
  We kneel its porch within,
Beneath those nail-pierced Hands which take
  Their vengeance upon sin.

Upheld to God, outstretched to men,
  How mighty their appeal !
Let but the grace be sought, ah, then
  How swift they are to heal !

The Cross belongs not to the past,
  Its virtue is not spent ;
Its shadow o'er the world is cast
  In this sweet Sacrament.

It lives—an ever-growing Tree,
  Its flowers never fade ;
The fruit of Immortality
  We gather in its shade.

"Tis Jesu's throne, a throne of Grace,
    He dwells with us, and still
His children seek their Lord's embrace
    Upon His altar-hill.

And seeking find :—Ah ! dearest Lord,
    Thus at Thy Cross we bow ;
Discerned, confessed, embraced, adored,
    Our All-in-all art Thou !

PALESTINE, May, 1875.

PRAYER.

'When ye pray say, Our Father.'

To rest beneath a Father's eye,
  Upon a Father's breast,—
This is the children's lot, and thus
  All praying souls are blest ;
They gaze upon a Father's face,
  A Father's voice they hear,
And praying lips are sweetly laid
  Against a Father's ear.

For prayer is just the child's caress,
  When cradled in the arms
Of Love Paternal ; this it is
  That comforts and that calms ;
But prayerless souls are comfortless,
  The victims of unrest,
Self-centred and dissatisfied,
  Unquickened and unblest.

From this, dear Lord, Thou savest us
    In teaching us to pray—
I thank Thee for the blessed words,
    More precious every day—
The children's prayer ; in teaching this
    Truly Thou teachest all ;
It makes the whole wide world a home,
    Life one long festival.

Oh, would that souls disconsolate,
    Self-weary, sick with sin,
Would pray this prayer, and lay them down
    A Father's arms within !
'Tis this that makes the burden light
    Of every grief and care ;
It ministers the balm that soothes
    The pangs of self-despair.

'Tis this that rallies souls beset
    And worsted in the strife ;
'Tis this that re-invigorates
    The sacramental life ;*
'Tis this that makes the feeble strong,
    That makes the dying brave,
The prayer that is a cradle-song
    Makes music at the grave.

* ' Semel abluimur Baptismate, quotidie abluimur oratione.
S. Augustine.

Lord, visit those who know not how
  In self-prostrating prayer
To fall before Thy mercy-seat,
  And find their solace there ;
Who bring no alabaster-box
  To break in homage meet,
No costly nard, no contrite tears,
  To bathe Thy blessed Feet.

Oh, win a prayer from prayerless lips,
  Make bright the souls so dim
Of sons who, when their Father speaks,
  Refuse to answer Him !
Oh, school the lips of praying men
  To do their work aright—
Their blissful, sacerdotal work,
  Till faith be lost in sight !

Thy Kingdom come ! Thy Will be done !
  So through the night we pray,
Till, scattered by the rising Sun,
  The shadows flee away ;
Then praise shall take the place of prayer,
  And toil shall end in rest,
And all Thy children everywhere
  Shall be for ever blest !

CORFU, June, 1875.

A LITANY OF OBSECRATION.

FATHER, listen to the crying
   Of the children at Thy knee ;
Jesu, Thou wilt own as brothers
   Those whose hearts appeal to Thee ;
To be called Thy friends and clients,
   Holy Spirit, make us meet ;
We salute Thee, we invoke Thee,
   By Thy Name of Paraclete ;
We confess Thee, we adore Thee,
   Consubstantial Trinity;
Visit us with Thy Salvation,
   Be Thyself our Jubilee !

By Thy blissful benediction,
   By Thy beautiful bequest—
' Peace I leave, My peace I give you,'
   And 'The peace-makers are blest,'—
Saviour, Master, we adjure Thee,
   Aid Thy Church so tempest-tost,
Re-awaken Sinai's thunder
   In the hush of Pentecost.
By Thy love, O Uncreated !
   Seeking a created home,

Through the Spirit's operation
   Cloistered in a Virgin's womb;
By the joy of kings and shepherds
   When Thine Eyes saluted them,
Brighter than the star that lingered
   O'er the roofs of Bethlehem;
By Thy Boyhood's constant vision
   Of a fast-approaching death;
By the memories that gather
   Round the hearth of Nazareth;
By Thy going forth to battle,
   When the Tempter strove with Thee;
By the long-protracted struggle,
   And the blood-bought victory;
When the blushing Moon beheld Thee
   Prostrate in a bloody sweat,
By the unimagined sorrows
   Of that night on Olivet;
By the Cross's proclamation
   Of a world-embracing love,
When the earth beneath Thee trembled,
   And the sky grew black above;
By Thy Rising and Ascending;
   By the long nine days' suspense;
By the Pentecostal Shower's
   Manifold magnificence;
On the bright baptismal waters
   By the Spirit's swift descent;

By the love, all love excelling,
   Of the Blessed Sacrament ;
Oh, by all Thou hast accomplished,
   And by all Thou hast endured,
May the bulwarks of Thy Sion
   Be triumphantly restored !
Hear, oh, hear us, we adjure Thee !
   Make Thy Church again to shine
With a beauty and a lustre
   Unmistakeably divine !
Crown Thy Bride, and may the children
   Of the Bride-chamber rejoice,
Folded to a Mother's bosom,
   Gladdened by a Father's voice !

Father, Thou wilt heed the crying
   Of the children at Thy knee ;
Jesu, Thou wilt own as brothers
   All who lift their hearts to Thee ;
Holy Ghost, Emancipator,
   Thee with confidence we greet,
For Thy consolations fail not,
   And Thy Name is Paraclete ;
Come to be our strong Salvation,
   Come to make our Jubilee,
Everlasting, Undivided,
   Consubstantial Trinity !

MONTE CASSINO, January, 1872.

A GOOD FRIDAY MEDITATION

I.

God, Thou art here,
I love Thee and I fear.

II.

I come to meditate on Death,
Life-giver, may Thy quickening breath
  My inspiration be ;
Oh, ponder what the Spirit saith,
    My soul, to thee !

III.

'Tis night—dark night—on Calvary,
  The Cross is very high ;
My straining eyes can scarcely see
  Beneath the blackened sky
The figure of the Crucified ;
    Ah me !
  For me He died.

For me ! for all !—still whiter grows
 That figure on the Rood ;
His life-blood (robe of purple) flows,
 Thus must His Spouse be wooed ;
The Royal Bridegroom claims the Bride,
  The Church
  For which He died.

And oh ! how dark my life, and dark
 Its future as its past,
But for His saving Passion ;—hark !
 The goal is reached at last ;
' 'Tis finishèd,' the Saviour cried ;
  Ah me !
  For me He died.

He speaks of work accomplished ; yes !
 His labours have an end,
The Risen Christ is strong to bless,
 Is mighty to befriend ;
And ever open is His Side,—
  My Home,
  For whom He died.

Thence flows the stream whose fountain-head
 Is in the sacred Heart,
For me the precious Blood was shed,
 I claim in it a part ;

That cleansing sacramental tide
      Heals me ;
   For this He died.

The night is past ; on Calvary
   Bright shines the Easter sun ;
For me He died, He lives for me,
   The Victory is won !
And Heaven's Gate is opened wide
      To me
   For whom He died.

IV.

Is this the vision that I see ?
    The Crucified,
    My God, my Guide,
Enthroned, triumphant, glorified !
   What joy for thee,
For thee, my soul, for whom He died !

To thee He speaks, as erst He spoke
    To souls distrest,
    And thou art blest
To whom these words are now addressed,
    ' Assume My yoke,
And learn of Me ; I give thee rest.'

V.

Dear Lord, since Thou hast died for me,
And by Thy Passion set me free
　　From sin's degrading thrall ;
My joy shall be to live for Thee,
　　My God, my All !

VI.

To God alway
My loving thanks I pay.

A THANKSGIVING.

'He hath put a new song in my mouth, even a thanksgiving unto our God.'

I THANK Thee, Lord, for all the hopes
　　That make the future fair,
I thank Thee for the memories
　　That interdict despair ;
I thank Thee for the lights and shades
　　Of life's fast-closing day ;
I thank Thee for the joys that live,
　　The griefs that die away.

I thank Thee for the Creed that grows
　　More precious every year ;
I thank Thee for the Voice that speaks
　　So musically clear ;
I thank Thee for the ' Peace, be still '
　　That calms the spirit's strife ;
I thank Thee for baptismal birth,
　　And sacramental life.

M

I thank Thee for the bread of tears,
   Its bitterness is sweet ;
I thank Thee for the witness-wounds
   In Hands and Side and Feet ;
I thank Thee for the discipline
   Of penance and of prayer,
And for the healing Cross that throws
   Its shadow everywhere.

Thine altar-sacrament reveals
   The depths of love divine,
Thy priestly Hands o'ershadow still
   The gifts of bread and wine ;
I thank Thee for that Gift of gifts,
   That legacy of love,
The one Oblation that endures,
   The Feast all feasts above.

I thank Thee for the holy Home
   Where all Thy children dwell,
The Church ! it is 'a wealthy place,'
   A rock-built citadel ;
And angel-guards and patron-saints
   Around the fortress stand ;
I thank Thee for their tutelage
   In yonder fatherland.

I thank Thee for the blessed Book
   And all its written lore ;
The Truth has made Thy children free,
   We know Whom we adore ;
I thank Thee for the stream of Grace
   That from Thy Throne descends,
I thank Thee for the Creed that speaks
   Of life that never ends.

I thank Thee for the love that binds
   These feeble hands to Thine,
Then bids them do a priestly work
   And bless the bread and wine ;
I thank Thee for the love that lets
   This feeble tongue declare
Thy pardon to the penitent
   Who kneels to Thee in prayer.

I thank thee, Lord, for all the hopes
   That make the future fair,
I thank thee for the memories
   That interdict despair ;
I thank Thee for the blessedness
   Of life's fast-waning day,
And treasure stored in that dear Land
   No longer far away.

But more than all I thank Thee, Lord,
　For Bliss that is Thine Own,
The Glory of Thy Diadem,
　Thy Sceptre and Thy Throne ;
Oh, 'tis a joy with rapture fraught
　That thrills the child-like heart,
To ponder Thy Beatitude—
　That Thou art what Thou art !

New Year's Day, 1876.

SONNETS.

THE THRONE OF SOLOMON.

'Moreover, the king made a great throne of ivory, and over-
laid it with pure gold.'

EACH winter is prophetical of spring.
A prophecy he wrought who made of old
A throne of ivory o'erlaid with gold,
A seat befitting an anointed king.
There Sheba's queen beheld him, wondering :
The wisdom God imparted and controlled
Empowered him her secrets to unfold,
And answer all her anxious questioning.
Foreshadowed by the seat of Solomon,
A royal throne more beautiful, more blest,
Hath God prepared for His Anointed Son—
The Maiden-Mother's undefilèd breast.
True sons were they of Sheba's pilgrim-queen
Who laid their gifts Christ's baby-hands between.

DISCIPLESHIP.

'Everyone that is perfect shall be as his master.'

Who follows Christ, upon the blood-stained stair
His feet must set; this is the homeward way,
Wherein to walk is evermore to say—
' Thy Will, not mine,'—the Great Forerunner's prayer :
Wherein to walk is evermore to bear
The Cross, pursuing Him, Whom to obey
Is to be sealed a victim day by day,
And evermore the crown of thorns to wear.
Our Aaron's censer yields its fragrance still,
Entrusted to their wounded hands who make
The Pure Oblation on His holy hill.
An alabaster-box, my heart, Lord, take,
Its emptiness with love's sweet ointment fill,
Then let me at Thy Feet kneel down and break.

PRIESTHOOD.

'The priesthood of the Lord is their inheritance.'

OF old stood Aaron in the Holiest Place ;
The glory-star above the mercy-seat
Had slain him with its lustre and its heat,
But for the incense-cloud that veiled his face.*
Grand prophecy of sacramental grace !
Now all are priests who firmly plant their feet
On holy ground, and offer what is meet,
Th' anointed Son unto the Sire's embrace.
The glory-star—it is the Father's smile ;
The mercy-seat—that Manhood without stain
Now glorified, but crucified erewhile,
Bejewelled with the wounds that still remain,
And show to simple souls and without guile
The glory of the sacrament of pain.

GENOA, 1879.

* Leviticus xvi. 13.

VITA VITÆ NOSTRÆ.

'To me to live is Christ.'

God's garden blossoms in a wilderness,
The Tree of Life is planted in a tomb,*
The Life of life springs from a virgin-womb,
From death emerges One who comes to bless
With gifts of life, our dying to redress,
Who feeds us in His Father's upper room
With living bread ; His Breath is a perfume,
His Face a sun, His Smile a warm caress.
O Life, of death the Death ! O conquering Love !
Too late, alas ! to Thine embrace I come,
And yield myself the vassal of Thy Will.
Thy Spirit's light and truth send from above,
And lead me to my many-mansioned home,
Those upper chambers on Thy holy hill.

SIENA, February, 1879.

* See Note L.

THE TEARS OF JESUS.

'With strong crying and tears learned He obedience by the things which He suffered ; and being made perfect, He became the Author of eternal salvation unto all them that obey Him.'

SHARP is the Cross, and Calvary is steep,
And tearful are the love-illumined Eyes
Of Him who hangs thereon and meekly dies
That sinners, love-constrained, may learn to weep.
The harvest of His Passion He must reap ;
Responsive to His travail-tears and cries
Forth from their graves sin-stricken souls arise,
The victims Hell is powerless to keep.
Christ is the Shepherd of His Father's sheep,
The Keeper of God's ransomed Israel,
Whose tear-filled, love-lit Eyes refuse to sleep
Till vanquished are the yawning Gates of Hell.
These precious relics shall my heart enshrine,
O Tears of Christ, all-human, all-divine !

BORDIGHERA, February, 1879.

THE WOUNDS OF JESUS.

'Faithful are the wounds of a friend.'

FIVE Witness-Wounds ! in each may be discerned
A mouth whose speech is lovely reticence,
Whose reticence impassioned eloquence,
Whereby entranced the hearts of men have yearned
Like Him to grow, Who on His death-bed turned
Right royally His bounty to dispense
To Dysmas wounded, won to penitence,
When by the world He wooed His love was spurned.
Pathetic speak those silent Wounds to me,
Faithful they are, and this their witness true—
'One lives Who loves thee unforsakingly ;
Like Him to grow, thou must be wounded too,
The heart must bleed that craves like His to be,
And bleeding hands alone His works may do.'

BETCHWORTH, April, 1879.

THE SMILES OF JESUS.

'Jesus rejoiced in spirit.'
'Show the light of Thy Countenance, and we shall be whole.'

THY Bliss, dear Lord, our human joy creates ;
But for the smile that lives upon Thy Face,
Forlorn we had not found one sunny place
In this dark world ; but now the Golden Gates
Stand ever open, and Thy gladness waits
On sorrow sanctified, when souls retrace
Their wandering steps, enkindled by Thy grace,
Whose joy Thy glad approval consecrates.
Thy Smiles outlive our tears ; there comes a day
When all shall know the joy of priests and kings,
And Thy dear Hand shall wipe all tears away.
Then shall Thy Smile discover many things,
Why laugh the hearts of children at their play,
Why skip the lambs, and why the skylark sings.

SIENA, February, 1879.

THE HOSPITALITY OF JESUS.

' And Jesus said, Make the men sit down.   Now there was much grass in the place.' *

With care the Feast Thou makest is prepared,
Not bread and fish alone, a grassy seat,—
And desert-grass means water cool and sweet,
And palm-tree shade ; for all Thy Love hath cared ;
Thy Hospitality no pains hath spared
To make the gift Thou givest all-complete ,
Thy Hands that break the bread have washed the
      feet ;
Thy Lips that bless the cup the thirst have shared.
Thyself dost minister to every guest,
And perfect is Thine every offering ;
Yet still, though perfect all, the last is best.
A shepherd-boy of old did truly sing
(Of all the songs he sang the loveliest)
' They nothing lack whom Thou art shepherding.

COLOGNE, September, 1880.

* See Note M.

A BOOK OF HALF-SONNETS.

A month,—to every day a text assigned:
It is an old device,—a method new
With measured words I tremblingly pursue,
Hoping that it may win approval kind
From lips that flatter not, tender and true.
Ah ! more to me thy blame than others' praise,
So long thy love hath blest my months and days.

I.

'If ye know these things, happy are ye if ye do them.'—
S. John. xiii. 17.

OUR days and months must, like the Church's year,
Recall that Life of labour that was rest—
Of all heroic lives the loveliest—
Which Jesus lived what time He sojourned here.
Still He abides, our Comrade and our Guest.
Ah ! life becomes a festival indeed
As day by day we learn to *live* our Creed !

II.

ADVENT.

'And He that sat upon the Throne said, Behold, I make all
things new.   And He said unto me, Write: for these words are
true and faithful.'—Apocalypse xxi. 5.

A FATHER'S love I know is love indeed,
His gracious purpose nothing can frustrate,
What *seems* is not what *is*,—wistful I wait
Till Jesus comes to verify my Creed,
My failing life to re-inaugurate.
Sweet are the words meanwhile, 'faithful and true,'
He comes ! He comes ! Who maketh all things new !

III.

ADVENT.

'There are so many kinds of voices in the world, and none of them is without signification.'—1 Corinthians xiv. 10.

ALL things their music yield,—the nights and days,
The psalmody of earth and sky and sea,
Bird-song and insect-hum,—all speak of Thee,
Each has a voice whose utterance is praise.
The Gospel-trumpets sound the Jubilee ;
One Voice there is, above all others heard
Throughout the ages, heralding the WORD.*

IV.

CHRISTMAS.

' And Jesus called a little child unto Him, and set him in the midst.'—S. Matthew xviii. 2.

THE filial life ! this is the life divine !
The child is evermore th' apostle true
Of Him Who what He sees His Father do
Does only, saying ' Not My will, but Thine.'
Such was the wisdom wherein Jesus grew.
Behold the Child the Father's love hath placed
For ever ' in the midst ' to be embraced !

* See Note N.

V.

EPIPHANY.

' And looking up to Heaven, He sighed, and saith unto him,
Ephphatha, that is, Be opened.'*—S. Mark vii. 34.

SPEAK, Lord, to ears and lips, to deaf and dumb,
Thine ' Ephphatha,'—to eyes that cannot see.
Hearing Thy Voice, Thy mouthpiece shall we be,
Seeing Thy Face, Thy mirror shall become ;
And so at length we shall resemble Thee.
Our hearts Thy word must pierce, Thy love must
    wound,
To make one music with Thine own attuned.

VI.

EPIPHANY.

' I will behold Thy presence in righteousness, and when I
awake up after Thy likeness I shall be satisfied with it.'—
Psalm xvii. 16.

' IN righteousness,'—so only can we go
Into the Presence-chamber, and behold
The Face of God ; so only be enrolled
Among the men of vision,—only so.
Thy likeness, Lord, in me Thy child unfold,
Bid me from sin arise, bid me awake,
Conformity shall satisfaction make.

* S. Ambrose, referring to this passage, calls Baptism the
' sacrament of Opening' (*apertionis mysterium*).

VII.

EPIPHANY.

'We all, beholding as in a glass the glory of the Lord, are
changed into the same image from glory to glory.'—2 Corinthians
iii. 18.

A MIRROR-FACE upturned, a crystal Sea,
On which a glory falls from heights unseen ;—
Such heights and depths of love man stands between
Above, beneath, 'tis God's Humanity
That mediates, nought else may intervene.
Self-revelation ! 'tis God's cherished plan,
His Image we behold, the Son of Man !

VIII.

EPIPHANY.

'Blessed are the pure in heart, for they shall see God.'—
S. Matthew v. 8.

MEN must be men the Son of Man to see,
Conformed to Him whose righteousness is love,
And day by day awakened from above
By the sweet Voice that whispers ' Follow me.'
Thus only God's beatitude we prove,
As day by day self-satisfaction dies,
And life is found to be ne victim's prize.*

* S. John xii. 24, 25.

IX.

LENT.

'The Father Himself loveth you.'—S. John xvi. 27.

GOD holds high festival when souls awake,*
And from their fevered sleep of sin arise,
Waked by the love-light of a Father's eyes,
A love that fails not, that can ne'er forsake.
Ah ! this is life,—that love to recognise
And make response ; there is no life but this,
A Father's love to know, a Father's kiss !

X.

LENT.

'The Well is deep.'—S. John iv. 11.

O LIPS inspired, although polluted, whence
Come words of truth, so little understood !
Deep is that Well, the water sweet and good,
Which from the Heart of God His Hands dispense
Whose water is God's wine, Whose wine His Blood.
With that dear penitent I too confess
Thy Well is deep, sweet Lord, yea, fathomless !

* 'Habet ergo Deus dies festos? Habet. Est enim ei
magna festivitas humana salus.'—ORIGEN.

XI.

LENT.

'The kingdom of God is within you.'—S. Luke xvii. 21.

THE heavens that encompass us are seen
By those alone within whose hearts Thy grace
Hath formed a mirror that reflects Thy Face ;
The kingdom is within them, they are clean.
Open to Thee, dear Lord, my door I place :
So may I gaze entranced for evermore
Upon the heavens through Thy opened door.

XII.

LENT.

'I am the Way, the Truth, and the Life ; no man cometh
unto the Father but by Me.'*—S. John xiv. 6.

THOU art the Way, because anointed Priest
And Victim of Humanity Thou art ;
The Truth art Thou, for Thine the Prophet's heart
From human error savingly released ;
Thou art the Life, empowered to impart
All that is Thine ;—a King because a Son,
Who for Thy brothers hast a birthright won.

* 'Hoc est, per Me venitur ; ad Me pervenitur ; in Me per-
manetur.'—S. AUGUSTINE.

XIII.

PASSIONTIDE.

'I have called you friends.'—S. John xv. 15.

THAT Love is ever crucified I see,
Yet unforsaking hastens to pursue ;
Faithful are Friendship's wounds, their witness true,
At length methinks it must triumphant be.
' Friends and not servants have I callèd you '—
Ah Princely Heart ! Thy Tenderness must win
All men at last from servitude to sin.

XIV.

PASSIONTIDE.

' Take My yoke upon you, and learn of Me . . . . My yoke
is easy and My burden is light.'—S. Matthew xi. 29, 30.

THE blessed burden that they bear bears them
Who, shouldering the Cross, the road pursue—
The royal road with Calvary in view—
Which to God's City leads, Jerusalem,
That City ever old and ever new !
Not hard the yoke, nor is the journey long
They share with Christ ; their Yokefellow is strong.

XV.

MAUNDAY THURSDAY.

'The Lord thy God in the midst of thee is mighty; He will save, He will rejoice over thee with joy; He will be silent in His love, He will joy over thee with singing.'—Zephaniah iii. 17.

'God in the midst;' so speaks the sanctus-bell;
Ecstatic silence follows still and deep,
For very joy we are constrained to weep,
That Presence soothes and stimulates as well.
'Tis thus a mother sings her babe to sleep;
And by her fragrant lips, when morning breaks,
The babe saluted smilingly awakes.

XVI.

GOOD FRIDAY.

'The great City which spiritually is called Sodom and Egypt where also our Lord was crucified.'—Apocalypse xi. 8.

Sodom and Egypt is the world, no less
Babel and Edom, whence the four roads meet
That make the Cross; a Sacrifice complete
Is offered there, and lo! the wilderness
Becomes a garden fruitful, fair and sweet.
Thus God reclaims His world, reconsecrates
His Paradise, and opes the Golden Gates.

XVII.

EASTER EVE.

'The sleep of a labouring man is sweet.'—Ecclesiastes v. 12.

THE Husbandman Divine is tasting now
The slumber sweet reserved for them who toil;
His bloody sweat hath rebaptized the soil
Whose thorns uprooted crowned His bleeding Brow.
A Conqueror He now divides the spoil.
'Twas for our sake the earth was cursed we know;*
And brings God's curse a blessing?—even so!

XVIII.

EASTER DAY.

'The serpent said unto the woman, Ye shall not surely die.'—
Genesis iii. 4.

UNWILLING servant of the King of kings,
The arch-deceiver purposing a lie,
Asserting this—'Ye shall not surely die,'
Deceives himself, and a true message brings.
Thus Satan is constrained to prophesy.
Life ever conquers death;—'among the dead
Why seek the Living?'—so an Angel said.

* Genesis iii. 17; cf. Galatians iii. 13.

XIX.

EASTER.

'Let us eat and be merry, for this my son was dead and is alive again; he was lost and is found.'—S. Luke xv. 23, 24.

'EAT and be merry,'—'tis the Father's voice;
His chambers all with merriment resound,
The Dead One lives again, the Lost is found.
'Tis meet that men and angels should rejoice.
The winding-sheet for all men is unwound;
Open and empty is His garden-grave
Who died, by death from death mankind to save.

XX.

ASCENSION DAY.

'I leave the world and go to the Father.'—S. John xvi. 28.

'I LEAVE the world;'—and are we then bereft?
Is that sweet Presence now at length withdrawn,
Whose glad return made of our Easter morn
A radiant festival? The tomb He left;
And leaves He now the world unblest, forlorn?
No! to the Father speaks a human Voice—
'All Mine are Thine;'—rejoice, my soul, rejoice!

XXI.

PENTECOST.

'There rose up Fire out of the Rock.'—Judges vi. 21.

CHRIST is that sheltering Rock, whence water sweet
To fertilize a barren world outflows ;
The watered desert blossoms as a rose
Beneath His Pilgrim-Bride's advancing feet.
But more than this did Pentecost disclose ;
When thereunto, a Pilgrim still, she came
Forth from that Rock upsprang an altar-flame.

XXII.

PENTECOST.

'All things are yours, and ye are Christ's, and Christ is
God's.'—1 Corinthians iii. 21, 23.

ALL things the members share with Christ the Head ;
Possest of Him, we are of all possest,
Sorrow is joy, and labour blissful rest,
If by His Spirit we be visited ;
We call His Father ' Father,' and are blest.
And oh ! what hospitality His Heart
Waits to dispense ; claim then, my soul, thy part.

XXIII.

PENTECOST.

'The Preacher, the Son of David, King in Jerusalem.'—
Ecclesiastes i. 1.

THERE is one Preacher, though so many preach,
One by Whose Lips the true prophetic word
Is ever uttered ; His the Spirit's sword,
Unsheathed to slay the lie, the truth to teach.
To David's Son is victory assured
Over all Philistines ;—Jerusalem
His City is, and His the Diadem.

XXIV.

PENTECOST.

' Upon one Stone shall be seven eyes.'—Zechariah iii. 9.

GOD's sanctuary-lamps are seven eyes
With rapture fixed upon one Altar-Stone,
One living Shrine, one sacramental Throne —
Enamoured with an ever fresh surprise
Of loveliness increasingly made known.
The seven Gifts are eyes for men to see
God's love revealed in Christ's Humanity.

XXV.

TRINITY SUNDAY.

'The Spirit of the Living Creature was in the wheels.'—
Ezekiel i. 20.
'God is a Spirit.'—S. John iv. 24.

THE wheels revolving may be clearly seen—
Wheel within wheel, 'tis these that meet men's eyes ;
The victims of delusion, they surmise
That this grand world is only a machine.
For them there waits a beautiful surprise,
When to the Centre driven by despair
They find a Living Spirit seated there.

XXVI.

CORPUS CHRISTI.

'For Thy Temple's sake at Jerusalem so shall kings bring
presents unto Thee.'—Psalm lxviii. 29.

CHRIST of the Temple of His Body spake ;
So speaks the Psalmist, of that Flesh and Blood,
Uplifted on the world-redeeming Rood,
Whereof His children evermore partake.
Thou, Prince of Salem, art our daily food ;
Born of a Royal House, our hearts we bring,
And lay them at Thy Feet, O Father-King !

XXVII.

Corpus Christi.

'We were eyewitnesses of His Majesty.'—2 Peter i. 16.

THE light that shone on Tabor lingers still,
Encompassing God's people as they pray,
And making midnight brighter than noonday
Upon the summit of His holy hill.
Ah ! nevermore that vision fades away ;
It crowns the Christian altar, where the Christ
Is still transfigured in the Eucharist.

XXVIII.

Michaelmas.

'Take heed that ye despise not one of these little ones ; for
I say unto you that in heaven their Angels do always behold the
Face of My Father which is in heaven.'—S. Matthew xviii. 10.

SWEET angel-eyes on all God's children rest
As tenderly as on one holy Maid
One happy Angel gazed, what time he said
'The Lord is with thee, Mary, thou art blest,'
And God His Darling in her bosom laid.
Sweet eyes are theirs who angel-like can trace
In every mother's child the Father's Face !

XXIX.

ALL SAINTS' DAY.

'Blessed are they which are called unto the marriage-supper
of the Lamb.'—Apocalypse xix. 9.

ONE constant service doth the Saints employ,
Whose seats around God's Throne are lifted up,
Filled with love's wine each heart—a golden cup
Raised to His lips—a minister of joy.
Him they adore with Whom they sit and sup ;
Him they entreat that all men may repair
To His parental Heart, and shelter there.

XXX.

ALL SOULS' DAY.

· All they that go down into the dust shall kneel before Him. '
— Psalm xxii. 30.

THEY whom we call 'the Dead' are worshippers ;
In silent homage at the Master's Feet
Entranced they kneel, and offer what is meet,
Love's self-oblation, fragrant as was hers
Whose love was sweeter than her nard so sweet.
They only live who love ; souls are not dead
Who in love-life are being perfected.

XXXI.

'Jesus said, It is finished.'—S. John xix. 30.

My toil unfinished leaves my task undone :
But He Who toiled and died sublimely said—
In death a Conqueror—' 'Tis finishèd ;'
For me He spake that word, that battle won.
Ah, all-achieving Lord ! Thou art my Head ;
When fruitless seems my life and bare of flowers,
This comfort holds—Thy Fruitfulness is ours !

NOTES.

NOTE A.

'The Dogma of S. John.'—p. 4.

I QUOTE the following words from Canon Westcott's masterly introduction to the Gospel of S. John in the Speaker's Commentary :—'It is admitted on all hands that his (S. John's) central affirmation, "the Word became Flesh," which underlies all he wrote, is absolutely new and unique. A Greek, an Alexandrine, a Jewish doctor, would have equally refused to admit such a statement as a legitimate deduction from his principles, or as reconcilable with them. The message completes and crowns "the hope of Israel," but not as "the Jews" expected. It gives stability to the aspirations of humanity after fellowship with God, but not, as philosophers had supposed, by "unclothing" the soul. S. John had been enabled to see what Jesus of Nazareth was, "the Christ" and "the Son of God :" it remained for him to bring home his convictions to others. The Truth was clear to himself : how could he so present it as to show that it gave reality to the thoughts with which his contemporaries were busied ? The answer is by using with necessary modifications the current language of the highest religious speculation, to interpret a fact, to reveal a Person, to illuminate the fulness of actual life. Accordingly he transferred to the region of history the phrases in which men before him had spoken of "the Logos,"—"the Word," "the Reason,"—in the region of metaphysics. S. Paul had brought home to believers the divine majesty of the glorified Christ : S. John laid open the unchanged majesty of "Jesus come in the flesh."

'It is characteristic of Christianity that it claims to be "the Truth." Christ spoke of Himself as "the Truth." God is revealed in Christ as "the only true (ἀληθινός) God." The message of the Gospel is "the Truth." This title of the Gospel is not found in the Synoptists, the Acts, or the Apocalypse ; but it occurs in the Catholic Epistles, and in the Epistles of S. Paul. It is specially characteristic of the Gospel and Epistles of S. John.

'According to the teaching of S. John, the fundamental fact of Christianity includes all that "is" in each sphere. Christ the Incarnate Word is the perfect revelation of the Father : as God, He reveals God. He is the perfect pattern of life, expressing in act and word the absolute law of love. He unites the finite and the infinite. And the whole history of the Christian Society is the progressive embodiment of this revelation.'—pp. xv. and xliv.

NOTE B.

'*Thine all-sustaining Eucharist
Thy Motherhood declares.*'—p. 8.

I AM anxious to vindicate an expression that is per-
haps open to criticism. It is, I think, clear, from the
statement of Genesis i. 27, that the mystery of sex
belongs not only to our race, but also to our nature.
Man is created in God's image, male and female, and
is part of that creation which is declared to be '*very
good*' (i. 31). But almost immediately we hear from the
lips of God a very different announcement: 'It is *not
good* that man should be alone;' and then woman is
taken out of man (ii. 23). This separation of the man
and the woman introduced, I apprehend, a condition
of things far from perfect, but better in one respect
than the condition which it superseded, because an
onward step in the direction of the best—of perfection.
Just as God in the mystery of creation holds His child
at arm's length (so to speak) in order that the child,
beholding and regarding Him, may be enamoured of
His loveliness, and make deliberately and intelligently
the response which His love demands, so it may be
necessary, if the distinction between the man and the
woman is to be rightly apprehended, upon which the
maintenance of right relations between them depends,
that they should be made to confront one another. The
separation, therefore, of Genesis ii. 23 would seem to
be preparatory to the perfected sacramental embrace
of which the Lord speaks, referring to this very passage,

o

in S. Matthew xix. 5 : 'And they twain shall be one flesh.'

In like manner the Manhood of the second Adam, 'the first-born of every creature,' was created both male and female, and, as the Fathers teach, from His Side, opened on the Cross, the second Eve was taken, His Bride, and the Mother of all living. The Manhood of Christ being perfect (not limited moreover by alliance with a human personality) includes a perfect woman-hood, and that womanhood a perfect motherhood. And this is what the separation wrought out upon the Cross discovers. Then, indeed, as the glorious consummation of the all-revealing Passion, woman was taken out of Man. The Church's Motherhood is derived from His.

This profound theological conclusion, which I cannot regard as in any way precarious, is supported by various expressions in Holy Scripture, and is at once suggested when we contemplate the Eucharistic mystery as a Communion-feast, wherein with His own substance God feeds, as with mother's milk, His 'little children' (S. John xiii. 33). S. James i. 18 is rightly translated in the Revised Version : 'Of His own will He brought us forth' (ἀπεκύησεν ἡμᾶς) ; the word used indicates an operation of the divine Motherhood. And in the opening vision of the Apocalypse the Son of Man is represented as 'girt about the paps with a golden girdle.' It is observable that the word used here (μαστὸς, not μαζὸς) signifies the woman's breast. Such passages, if the interpretation suggested be the right one, throw additional light on many others ; e.g. Isaiah lxvi. 13 ; S. Matthew xxiii. 37. The Hypostatic Union is the complete recovery and reconstruction of humanity, and the reconciliation of all antinomies. From this flows the mystical

union of Christ and the Church, the sacramental union
of Christ and the regenerate soul. The Bridegroom and
the Bride, though distinct, are not separate.

The Motherhood of Christ, like all the mysteries of the
Incarnation, points to a larger mystery in the Inner Life
of God. S. Gregory Nazianzen speaks of the Ever-
Blessed Trinity as the Eternal Virgin : Πρώτη παρθένος
ἐστιν ἀγνὴ Τριάς ; that Virgin is also the Eternal Mother.
The same idea finds musical expression in one of Mr. Aubrey
de Vere's ' May Carols,' a hymn for Trinity Sunday :—

> ' Prime Virgin, separate and sealed,
>   Nor less of social love the root ;
> Dimly in lowliest shapes revealed,
>   Entire in every attribute.'

It is needless to say that to apprehend in any measure
these truths concerning God and Christ is to be safe-
guarded against errors which are always liable to creep
in, whenever the cultus of our Lady is not rigorously
submitted to the tests which are furnished by a profound
and accurate theological science.

I am glad to find my meaning beautifully expressed
by Mr. Jukes in the following passage, which I had not
seen when I prepared the above note, though I know not
for how much of the vision that has opened to me of the
Motherhood of God (and for much besides) I am indebted to him :—

' One like unto the Son of Man walks in the midst
of the seven golden candlesticks, in priestly robes ; for
is He not the Priest, whose office is to keep alive the
fire, and trim the lights in God's sanctuary ; but showing
the woman's breast, for in the Lord the man is not without the woman nor the woman without the man, made

again, like Adam unfallen, where there is neither Jew nor Greek, nor male nor female, but a new creature and a new man in Christ Jesus. This is not the form in which the Son of Man is seen at first, for to redeem us He took our likeness, 'the likeness of sinful flesh,' and was circumcised upon the eighth day, that so, sharing the shame of our divided nature, He might bear its curse, and heal the breach, and through death bring us back in and for Himself, again to bear the undivided image of Him who formed man in His likeness.'—('The New Man,' p. 34.)

Let me add the testimony of one of the most thoughtful of modern preachers.

Mr. Robertson, commenting on Galatians iii. 28, understands S. Paul's words ' neither male nor female ' to signify *neither to the exclusion of the other.* He insists on the fact that in the Humanity of Christ 'there is nothing distinctive, limited, or peculiar.' 'His Heart,' he says, 'had in it the blended qualities of both sexes.' And again, ' There was in Him the woman-breast as well as the manly brain all that was most manly, and all that was most womanly.'—(Sermons, second series, xviii.)

I may mention a lovely book which is not as well known as it deserves to be, in which the idea of the Motherhood of Christ recurs again and again : ' Sixteen Revelations of Divine Love, showed to a Devout Servant of our Lord, called Mother Juliana, an anchorite of Norwich, who lived in the days of King Edward the Third.' London : S. Clarke, 1843.

NOTE C.

*' There shall be an heap of corn in the earth, high
upon the hills.'*—Psalm lxxii. 16.

> *' Long since the Psalmist-seer foretold*
> *That high upon the hills*
> *God's Corn should grow, and now behold,*
> *His promise He fulfils!'*—p. 17.

'A CLOUD of Rabbinical tradition hovers round⁀the
passage, and helps to frame it, that we may see it in
this (the sacramental) aspect. Besides the rendering
of the Targum given above, the following may be cited.
In the Midrash Coheleth, a comment on Ecclesiastes,
it is said that, as Moses caused manna to come down
from heaven, so Messiah shall be " a cake of corn upon
the earth." Rabbi Jonathan, in his Targum, reads,
" There shall be a sacrifice of bread upon the earth, on
the head of the mountains of the Church." And this
is further explained in the Sepher-Kibucim to the effect
that in the days of Messiah there shall be a cake of
corn lifted in sacrifice over the heads of the priests in
the Temple. Herein, most naturally, the commentators
see the Elevation of the Host, that primeval rite of the
Divine Liturgy wherein He Who is the substantiating
Bread, the Memorial Sacrifice, the Corn of mighty men,
is uplifted in oblation to the Father, Himself the Victim
and Himself the Priest.

'Again we may find a more literal fulfilment of the
prophecy in the events of the Gospel history, wherein
He who is the Bread of Life is seen so often " like a

young hart upon the mountains." In the temple on
Moriah, in the place of His first preaching, in the scene
of many an hour of prayer, in the Transfiguration, the
Crucifixion, the Ascension, again and again His feet are
beautiful on the mountains.

'Thrice for us the Word Incarnate high on holy hills
    was set,
Once on Tabor, once on Calvary, and again on Olivet :
Once to shine, and once to suffer, and once more as King
    of kings,
With a merry noise ascending, borne by cherubs on
    their wings.'

NEALE *and* LITTLEDALE,

'*Commentary on the Psalms,*' vol. ii. p. 407.

NOTE D.

'*My lips still hunger for Thy kiss
Touched by Thy coal of fire.*'—p. 29.

THERE is an interesting section of Dr. Pusey's great
work on 'The Doctrine of the Real Presence from the
Fathers,' touching the coal in Isaiah's vision regarded as
a type of the Holy Eucharist. I quote only a small
portion.

    From the Liturgy of S. James :—

    'The Lord bless us and make us worthy to take with
the pure "tongs" of our hands the fiery Coal, and to place
it on the mouths of the faithful, for the cleansing and
purifying of their souls and bodies, now and ever.'

And more at length, in the Liturgy of S. Cyril : —

'As Thou didst cleanse the lips of Thy servant Isaiah the Prophet, when one of the Seraphim took with the forceps a live coal off the altar, and came to him, and said to him, "Behold this hath touched thy lips, and thine iniquity shall be taken away, and all thy sins purged," so also do to us poor sinners, Thy wretched servants. Vouchsafe to sanctify our souls, our bodies, our lips, and hearts ; and give us that true Coal, which giveth life to our souls, bodies, and spirits, that is, the holy Body and precious Blood of Thy Christ ; not to our condemnation, nor that we should incur judgment.'

Renaudot says generally :—

'That coal also whereby in the vision the lips of Isaiah were touched and purified, is commonly said, in the prayers of the Easterns, to have been a type of the Eucharist ; and it is often said in their hymns which are sung at the distribution, that mortals receive fire in bread through the communion of the mysteries.'

S. John Damascene :—

'Wherefore with all fear and a pure conscience and unwavering faith, let us approach ; and it shall be to us in every respect, according as we believe, nothing doubting. Let us honour it with all purity both of soul and body. For it is twofold. Let us approach it with a burning desire, and placing our hands in the form of a cross, let us receive the Body of the Crucified ; and having signed eyes and lips and brow, let us receive the Divine Coal, that the fire of our longing, having received the enkindling of the Coal, may consume our sins, and enlighten our hearts, and that by the presence of that

Divine fire, we may be enkindled and deified. Isaiah saw the coal ; but coal is not mere wood, but wood united with fire ; so too, the bread of the Communion is not mere bread, but united to the Divinity ' (pp. 128-130.)

NOTE E.

' *The sick room has its sacrament.*'—p. 53.

I QUOTE the following from one whose memory is enshrined in many hearts, the late Bishop of Brechin :—

'The unction of the sick is the lost pleiad of the Anglican firmament. One must at once confess and deplore that a distinctly Scriptural practice has ceased to be commanded in the Church of England.'

And again :—

'The Church of England acted more in conformity to its declared adherence to antiquity, by appointing, in the first instance, a service for the anointing of the sick in her first English Prayer-book. This was among the losses in those unhappy times just before the accession of Mary, and although everything of that earlier liturgy was praised by those who removed it, it has never been restored. Since, however, the Visitation of the Sick is a private office, and uniformity is required only in the public offices, there is nothing to hinder the revival of the Apostolic and Scriptural custom of anointing the sick, whensoever any devout person may desire it. It is, indeed, difficult to say on what principle it could be refused. The rite was restored by the non-juring

Bishops. Meanwhile, until it can be generally restored, it may be observed that it was never considered necessary to salvation, as is formally laid down by S. Thomas. It was rather a privilege of the devout.'—(' Explanation of the Thirty-nine Articles,' pp. 465, 474.)

The following passage from the 'Institution of a Christian Man' declares plainly the mind of the Church of England at the Reformation period :—' All Christian men should repute and account the said manner of anointing among the other sacraments of the Church, forasmuch as it is a visible sign of an invisible grace : whereof the visible sign is the anointing with oil in the Name of God; which oil (for the natural properties belonging unto the same) is a very convenient thing to signify and figure the great mercy and grace of God, and the spiritual light, joy, comfort, and gladness which God poureth out upon all faithful people, calling upon Him by the inward unction of the Holy Ghost. And the grace conferred in this sacrament is the relief and recovery of the disease and sickness wherewith the sick person is then diseased and troubled, and also the remission of his sins if he be then in sin.'

The thought has much to recommend it which discovers in the anointing of our Lord at Bethany on the eve of His Passion, ' for His Burial,' a foreshadowing of this sacrament, as the first miracle was of the Eucharist, and the washing of the Apostles' feet of Absolution.

NOTE F.

'The Spirit of God is the spirit of man.'—p. 72.

I QUOTE, on a subject of surpassing interest, a few sentences from the sections of Martensen's great work on 'Christian Dogmatics,' which treat of the Procession of the Holy Ghost :—

'What Christ is in unity, the Spirit is in manifoldness. The design of the world is ideally accomplished in Christ : but it is through the Spirit that the one Christ obtains a place in the manifoldness of souls, and that the kingdom of God comes in the world. Here also is the Spirit the heavenly Master-builder, Who moulds the fulness of the Son into a temple of glory ; Who models and prepares the manifold natural idiosyncrasies of men, and the distinctive peculiarities of nations, into an organ for the one Christ.'

'As the Son did not reveal Himself fully until He became Man in the act of His Incarnation, so the Spirit does not fully manifest Himself until He comes not only as a temporary visitor, but as taking up a permanent abode, and forming an abiding union with mankind ; until He becomes the Spirit working in Christ's kingdom. It is only as *the Spirit of Christ* that the Holy Ghost can enter upon an abiding union with mankind. When the ideal union of the Divine nature with pure and sinless human nature was accomplished, when the Mediator between God and the kingdom of God had come, then only could the kingdom itself advance in power, then only could that genera

union of the Divine nature with sinful human nature be
accomplished, which is the copy or fac-simile of the
union of these natures in Christ. In Christ dwells the
fulness of the Godhead bodily; in Christ the union of
the two natures is such that the human nature possesses
no individuality apart from or before its union with the
Divine. But in the case of the Spirit, human souls
possess a natural and earthly individuality, apart from
and before their union with Him; and they need to be
transformed by the Holy Ghost, by little and little, into
the image of that perfection which belongs naturally and
essentially to Christ. While, however, this union of the
Spirit with sinful humanity is not precisely the same as
that which took place in the Incarnation, but is an
inhabitation, it is none the less a permanent, yea, an
indissoluble union. For as the union of natures in the
person of Christ can never be dissolved, but must con-
tinue through eternity, so, in virtue of the mediatorial
office of Christ, the Holy Ghost dwells for ever in the
kingdom of Christ.'

'All that the Spirit moulds is after the pattern of
Christ; and, speaking after the manner of man, we may
say, that as the human artificer regards in every work
some eternal and ideal pattern which is ever in his
mind, and embodies this his fundamental thought in
his manifold productions, so the Holy Spirit, the great
invisible Master-builder and Artificer of the temple, has
ever before Him the model and pattern of Christ, and
does nothing but what He seeth the Son do. But
inasmuch as the Spirit ever moulds human nature according to the one original type, yet into ever new forms,
ever new repetitions and varieties, He reveals Himself as
the Spirit of *freedom,* Who displays eternal truth. The

Principle of free development, continually creating the new upon earth, He renews and restores to youth and vigour the life of Christ in individual souls, and in the entire kingdom of Christ; He moulds the Christian doctrine and worship into new forms; He devises and finds out new means and plans for the spread of the kingly empire of Christ. He, the holy, ever-present Principle of Providence, reveals Himself as the Paraclete, Who on the one hand convinces the world of sin, of righteousness and of judgment, and on the other hand as the Comforter, not only of individual souls, but of the Church, wherein all the promises of history find their accomplishment. As the ever-present Principle of renewal and of living development, He proves Himself the Spirit of *power*: and thus through Him the kingly dominion of Christ never dies away, never grows old.'

'There is no operation of the Spirit in the Christian fellowship which is not in reality a display of Christ's working—"He shall take of Mine and shew it unto you;" and, conversely, there is no act of Christ's which is not carried on by the Spirit, "for no one can say that Jesus Christ is Lord but by the Holy Ghost." This natural and simultaneous working of the Lord and of the Spirit is manifested in the establishment, the maintenance and the perfecting of the Church.'—('Christian Dogmatics,' Eng. Tr., pp. 330-335.)

NOTE G.

' The lost are found, and all are blest.'—p. 92.

AT a time when we have so much reckless writing on both sides of an anxious controversy, it is a pleasure to be able to quote an illustrious author whose breadth, culture, sobriety, and singularly disciplined enthusiasm for all things lofty and lovely, invest his words with no small measure of authority :—

' Let us submit,' writes Dean Church, ' to the conditions of our state and of our knowledge ; we, at least, who in the tempest and confusions of the world have as our one supreme guiding light the manifestation, the words of the Son of God. Who shall say that, though we must greatly fear, we may not also greatly hope, even if we are met by awful certainties, if we dare not say more than He has said? We cannot tell what is between the grave and the judgment, but we know that the living God is there, very terrible, very pitiful, very just, who leads His creatures by ways they know not to the end which only He knows. We may be sure that He will set right in His own way the inequalities of this world. We may be sure that all who seek Him in truth shall one day find Him, for He has said so. We may be sure that everyone in every nation who feareth Him and worketh righteousness is accepted with Him, for His accredited apostle has said so. Is the righteousness of God too small a thing to trust to, unless we can say in detail how it is to be carried out? Are " the multitude of His mercies," to use a favourite phrase of the Psalms, the " multitude of His mercies" to which saint and penitent must alike appeal—are they too stinted, too straitened, that we cannot commit to them all the infinite issues of human life, which move our fellow-feeling, our pity, our sympathy? Can *we* be so compassionate and so just, and cannot we trust Him to be so, unless He shows us how? Can we not trust Him, in silent and awful expectation, with the work of His own hands, sure that He will not despise it—sure that under the shadow of His wings all the countless multitude of His creatures, from the highest to the lowest, the worst and the best, shall find His perfect truth—sure that each soul will receive what it ought to receive, and will be dealt with by infinite goodness and unerring justice.'—(' Human Life and its Conditions,' p. 123.)

NOTE II.

'*A May Day Song.*'—p. 104.

THE time has surely come when her children should, in the name of their Mother, very earnestly rebut the accusation so commonly brought against the Church of England, that she withholds from the blessed Virgin Mary, whose blessedness all generations of Christian men are bound to declare, the love and veneration which are her due. At the same time, I am anxious, for my own part, to disavow no less earnestly any sympathy with the modern devotional extravagances, so common in countries subject to the Roman obedience, in connection with the Month of Mary. Whether a special observance of that sweet month, when Nature herself takes up her parable in the interests of Grace, and

strikes so tenderly her harp of many strings, may or
may not with much propriety be recommended to
English Catholics, I leave it to others to decide. Under
the pressure of a very legitimate apprehension, we are
in some danger, I think, of failing to realise the true
position of the Mother of God in the Divine economy ;
and if this be so, not only is the glory of womanhood
obscured, but the intelligent acceptance of the supreme
mystery of the Incarnation is imperilled. It is important
that we should give *devotional* expression to all that is
involved in the great theological symbol of the Council
of Ephesus—θεοτόκος—to which, by God's mercy, the
Church of England is fully committed. And this is no
doubt the best safeguard against the misconceptions
and excesses of which we do well to beware. That
Cardinal Newman is alive to their dangerous tendency
his own words have made abundantly clear. 'There is,'
he says, 'a healthy devotion to the blessed Mary, and
there is an artificial ; it is possible to love her as a
Mother, to honour her as a Virgin, to seek her as a
Patron, and to exalt her as a Queen, without any injury
to solid piety and Christian good sense. I cannot help
calling this the English style.'—(' Letter to Dr. Pusey,'
p. 105.) But we still wait in vain to hear an authoritative
voice raised in repudiation and condemnation of the
' extravagances ' against which he protests. An earnest
observance of the month in which Spring and Summer
meet, as an act of rejoicing and sustained homage to
the love which the Incarnation discovers, and marked by
the fervour wedded to sobriety which is a characteristic
of the higher forms of English religious life, might per-
haps be our best protection against those untheological
developments and the practices to which they give rise,

which cannot but be a matter of regret to all well-instructed Catholics.

That the devotion and veneration, to which my little 'Song' gives most inadequate expression, are not alien to the mind of the Church of England, may be inferred from the fact that she has in her calendar consecrated five days to 'Our Lady,' to be observed in loving remembrance of her Conception, Nativity, Annunciation, Visitation, and Purification. And appeal may be made to the great representative Anglican divines—*e.g.* Bishop Andrewes makes mention in his private devotions of 'the all holy, undefiled, and more than blessed Mary, Mother of God and Ever-Virgin.' And Bishop Pearson writes :—' It was her own prediction, *From henceforth all generations shall call me blessed*; but the obligation is ours to call her, to esteem her so. If Elizabeth cried out with so loud a voice, *Blessed art thou among women*, when Christ was but newly conceived in her womb : what expressions of honour and admiration can we think sufficient now that Christ is in heaven, and that Mother with Him ! Far be it from any Christian to derogate from that special privilege granted her, which is incommunicable to any other. We cannot bear too reverend a regard unto the Mother of our Lord, so long as we give her not that worship which is due unto the Lord Himself. Let us keep the language of the primitive Church : let her be honoured and esteemed, let Him be worshipped and adored.' (' The Creed,' art. iii. p. 319. Oxford ed. 1857.) Among more modern writers it is difficult to make a selection, so many are the passages that speak of Mary's beauty and beatitude. Wordsworth's sonnet, however, is too lovely to be omitted :—

' Mother! whose virgin bosom was uncrost
   With the least shade of thought to sin allied ;
   Woman ! above all women glorified,
   Our tainted nature's solitary boast :
   Purer than foam on central ocean tost ;
   Brighter than eastern skies at daybreak strewn
   With fancied roses, than the unblemished moon
   Before her wane begins on heaven's blue coast :
   Thy image falls to earth.   Yet some, I ween,
   Not unforgiven the suppliant knee might bend,
   As to a visible power, in which did blend
   All that was mixed and reconciled in thee
   Of mother's love with maiden purity,
   Of high with low, celestial with terrene !'

Keble's many verses, expressive of the tenderest
devotion to 'the Spotless Mother,' are too numerous to
quote. They have been collected in an article by
Cardinal Newman ("Essays Critical and Historical,'
vol. ii. pp. 436-440), without, however, any reference to
one of the most beautiful of all, 'Mother out of Sight'
('Miscellaneous Poems,' p. 254), which deserves to be
coupled with the 'Ave Maria' hymn in 'The Christian
Year,' and that for Easter Day in the 'Lyra Innocen-
tium.' Dr. Pusey, in his 'Eirenicon,' speaks forcibly
of the not unreasonable fear by which 'our hearts have
been cramped' with regard to the blessed Virgin. 'It
is not,' he says, 'the amount of love for the Mother of
our Redeemer and our God (how could it be?), but the
mode of its expression, to which any of us have objected.'
And he goes on to speak touchingly and truly of the
'yearning towards her in the English Church,' by
reference to writers of more than one theological school.
'Part ii. pp. 411-419.)

Bishop Forbes has a beautiful passage, in which he speaks of the unfortunate results of this fear, engendered by 'the exaggerated language of Roman divines' in many devout minds. 'They have shrunk,' he says, 'from looking the doctrine concerning her fairly in the face. They have not allowed their minds to dwell on the incomparable singularity, on the incommunicable prerogative of Divine maternity. While they freely dwell on the gifts of God in other saints, in the patriarchs under the old law for instance, they shrink from resting on the sweet and holy images which surround the name of Mary. This is in every way wrong. A theology that is afraid of possible consequences is sure to err. We must state the absolute truth, and leave consequences to God. To eliminate from our moral theology the idea of the blessed Virgin, is to strip it of some of its most delicate bloom. What does not civilisation, what does not woman owe to the sublime and tender conception of Mary, which has done more to tame the rude social life of Europe in the middle ages than any other one idea! And what more constraining motive to purity of soul, next of course to the thought of Him Who is the great Exemplar of all virtues, can there exist than the idea of such perfect spotless womanhood as a grateful Christendom recognises in our Lady! But there is a still more serious thought. After making every allowance for the reaction against the distressing language of certain popular Roman devotions, there is a danger lest the shrinking from a due appreciation of the dignity of the Mother may not generate an imperfect belief in the Divine personality of the Son, and no error is so deadly as that which seeks to touch the person of Jesus.'— ('Thirty-nine Articles,' p. 31.)

With reference to the civilising and refining effects of the mediæval devotion to the Maiden-Mother, of which the Bishop speaks, I would refer to an unprejudiced witness, Mr. Lecky, who, in his 'History of European Morals,' dwells upon it earnestly (3rd edition, vol. ii. p. 367). And a recent writer in the 'Spectator,' reviewing Mr. Aubrey de Vere's ' May Carols,' writes as follows :—' Many eyes are turned towards the home at Nazareth even among those not professedly Christian, and students who desire to understand the power of the Gospel as a social force constraining all who come within knowledge of it, are roused by their very denial of revelation to examine the historical facts of the Christian story. . . . Who can calculate how large a part the cult of Mary had in establishing the European respect for women and reverence for the family hierarchy? It is the Semitic crown which completes the Aryan civilisation, and we confess we see with alarm any treason to that ideal of womanly life which has been maintained by Christian masters, in whatever art.'—(' Spectator,' September 3, 1881.)

' In the midst are the damsels playing with the timbrels '—so sings the Bride of Christ in the great Pentecost Psalm. And of that virgin-choir, beside the crystal sea, Mary—the true Miriam, our Elder Sister—is the acknowledged leader. By her alone has the aspiration of the woman-poet been perfectly realised :—

' May I reach
That purest heaven, be to other souls
The cup of strength in some great agony,
Enkindle generous ardour, feed pure love,
Beget the smiles that have no cruelty,

Be the sweet presence of a good diffused,
And in diffusion ever more intense ;
So shall I join the choir invisible,
Whose music is the gladness of the world.'

NOTE I.

' The royal-hearted Athanase.' *—p. 141.

I QUOTE the following eloquent words of one to whose
friendship I owe much. Speaking of S. Athanasius,
Dr. Bright says : 'His glorious career illustrates "the
incredible power of an orthodox faith, held with inflexible
earnestness, especially when its champion is an able and
energetic man." One is struck with the variety of gifts
and unity of aim which it exhibits. The infidel historian
deemed him fit to rule an empire, and obviously he had
to the fullest extent the power of dealing with men ; yet
he was publicly called for as "the ascetic" at his election,
and in exile he was a model of monastic piety. If he
is great as a theologian, and intensely given to Scripture
and sacred studies. he is "pre-eminently quick in seeing
the right course, and full of practical energy in pursuing
it." He is as kindly in his judgments of Liberius, and
Hosius, and the Council of Ariminum, as if he were not
the bravest of confessors. He can make allowance for
the difficulties of Semi-Arians, and recognise their real
" brotherhood" with himself. " Out of the strong comes
forth sweetness." It is this union of inflexibility and

---

* ' And royal-hearted Athanase,
With Paul's own mantle blest.'
LYRA APOSTOLICA.

discretion, of firmness and charity, this manysidedness
as a pattern for imitation, which makes him emphatically
Athanasius *the Great*. And wherever we find him—confronting opponents, baffling conspirators, biding his time
in Gaul or Italy, turning his hour of triumph to good
account for his flock, calling on them in the hour of
deadliest peril to praise the Everlasting Mercies, burying
himself in cells and dens of the earth, bearing honour
and dishonour with the same kingliness of soul, uniting
the freshness of early enthusiasm with the settled
strength of heroic manhood, writing, preaching, praying,
suffering,—he is enkindled and sustained throughout by
one clear purpose.

'What lay closest to his heart was not formula,
however authoritative ; no Council, however œcumenic.
His zeal for the Consubstantiality had its root in his
loyalty to the Consubstantial. He felt that in the
Nicene dogma were involved the worship of Christ and
the life of Christianity. The inestimable creed which he
was said to have composed in a cave at Trèves, is his
only in this sense, that, on the whole, it sums up his
teaching ; but its hymn-like form may remind us that
his maintenance of dogma was a life-long act of devotion. The union of these two elements is the lesson of his
life, as it was the secret of his power ; and by virtue of it,
as has been well said, although again and again it is
Athanasius contra mundum, yet Athanasius is in truth
the immortal, and ever in the end prevails. " Hæc est
victoria quæ vincit mundum, Fides nostra."'—(' History
of the Church,' 2nd edit. p. 148.)

NOTE K.

' And many another name bestae,
Wise Clement, lofty Origen,
Theirs is the honour due to men
Whose intellect is sanctified.'—p. 142.

MUCH has been written of late years about the saints
and doctors of Alexandria, and its celebrated Catechetical
School. I content myself with one sentence from a sermon
by Dr. Liddon, which concisely and beautifully expresses
what seems to me to be the first of many lessons that we
should learn from them :—' The great Alexandrians who
baptized the Platonic philosophy would have bidden us
of to-day welcome and christen the critical and scientific
spirit.'—(' University Sermons,' second series, p. 11.)

NOTE L.

' The Tree of Life is planted in a tomb.'—p. 168.

' THE place of a skull'—Golgotha or Calvary—is men-
tioned by all the Evangelists. Whether the tradition that
the Cross was planted in Adam's grave be true or not, it
certainly (like so many other legends *) points to a truth.
The world *is* a sepulchre, the sepulchre of Adam and of
Adam's race. The second Adam has entered this
sepulchre, passed through it, left it behind Him, and
the gate through which He rose in triumph remains open
to all who will follow in His steps.

* *E.g.* S. Veronica. *See* p. 128.

NOTE M.

' *The hospitality of Jesus.'*—p. 172.

IT cannot be doubted that the miracle of the feeding—
the only one recorded by all four Evangelists—was
strictly preparatory to the institution of the Eucharist.
It took place in all probability on the Thursday preceding
the memorable Sabbath, when in the great synagogue
of Capernaum our Lord preached the sermon on the
Bread of Life, recorded in S. John vi. immediately after
the account of the miracle. His every action on this occasion would seem to be an anticipation of what was after-
wards enacted with still greater solemnity in the Upper
Chamber, and is renewed at every celebration of the
Holy Mysteries. He took the loaves into His hands,
looked up to heaven, blessed, brake, and gave to the
disciples: then followed the orderly distribution through
their ministry to the seated multitude. The supply was
more than abundant; the fragments were sufficient to
furnish a second meal which would be required before
they reached their homes. And it should be remembered
that the lesson was emphasized by the working of a
similar miracle on another occasion. As these two
miraculous feedings foreshadow the Eucharist, so do
the two cleansings of the Temple—in reality no less
miraculous—foreshadow the Day of Judgment. So Joseph,
interpreting Pharaoh's dream to him, accounts for the
repetition of a Divine action :—' For that the dream was
doubled twice, it is because the thing is established by
God, and God will shortly bring it to pass.'—Genesis
xli. 32.

NOTE X.

' One Voice there is, above all others heard
Throughout the ages, heralding the Word.'— p. 176.

S. PAUL teaches us that Nature no less than Grace is
sacramental:—'The invisible things of Him from the
creation of the world are clearly seen, being understood
by the things that are made, even His eternal power
and Godhead' (Romans i. 20). 'All *things* in the
world' (to quote Stier) 'are, after their kind, only
variously embodied words of the Creator;' the sacramental shadows, in truth, cast by 'the invisible things,'
the spiritual realities which are out of sight. It is thus
God ever veils that he may reveal Himself. Creation is
a sacramental veil,[*] and, therefore, an authentic revelation of the mind and character of God, needing, however, to be interpreted by the all-revealing 'sacrament of
godliness,' the Incarnation. This is the master-key that
unlocks all mysteries. Truly has it been said by a
thoughtful writer:—'The counter-agent of materialism
is not idealism, but sacramentalism.' And he proceeds
to explain his meaning thus :—'Science has acquired a
new dignity for matter by the exhibition of its intimacy
with spirit. The loveliness of its forms and colours, the
wonder of its versatility, the mystery of its strange
sympathies and antipathies, are for ever haunting us
with the suggestion that matter is not what it seems.
But such suggestions have been long anticipated and
confirmed by the sacramental system, in whose light we
see the material order to be another aspect only of the

[*] *See the poem on Baptism, p. 58.*

spiritual, which is gradually revealing itself through material concealment, in the greater and the lesser Christian sacraments which radiate from the Incarnation, and in all the types, and parables, and symbolisms of nature, and the sacraments of storm and calm, and of the sunset and of the star-rise, and in every flash of an eye, or flush of a cheek, or pulse of a hand, that is, in its degree, the material instrument of spiritual communion. And so—

> " The whole round earth is every way
> Bound by gold chains about the feet of God." '

J. R. ILLINGWORTH,

' *Sermons preached in a College Chapel,*' p. 173.

LONDON : PRINTED BY
SPOTTISWOODE AND CO., NEW-STREET SQUARE
AND PARLIAMENT STREET